THE BEACH HOUSE

A **KISSING BOOTH** NOVELLA

BETH REEKLES

PENGUIN BOOKS

PENGUIN BOOKS

UK | USA | Canada | Ireland | Australia
India | New Zealand | South Africa

Penguin Books is part of the Penguin Random House group of companies
whose addresses can be found at global.penguinrandomhouse.com.

www.penguin.co.uk
www.puffin.co.uk
www.ladybird.co.uk

Ebook first published by Penguin Books 2019
Paperback first published by Penguin Books 2021

001

Set in 11/17 pt Palatino LT Std
Typeset by Jouve (UK), Milton Keynes
Printed and bound in Great Britain by Clays Ltd, Elcograf S.p.A.

The authorized representative in the EEA is Penguin Random House Ireland,
Morrison Chambers, 32 Nassau Street, Dublin D02 YH68

A CIP catalogue record for this book is available from the British Library

ISBN: 978-0-241-51246-3

All correspondence to:
Penguin Books
Penguin Random House Children's
One Embassy Gardens, 8 Viaduct Gardens
London SW11 7BW

PENGUIN BOOKS

THE BEACH HOUSE

Beth Reekles penned her novel *The Kissing Booth* when she was fifteen and began uploading it to story-sharing platform Wattpad, where it accumulated over 19 million reads. She was signed by Random House UK at the age of seventeen, and was offered a three-book deal while studying for her A Levels. Beth now works in IT, having graduated from Exeter University with a physics degree, and has had five books published with Penguin Random House Children's: *The Kissing Booth*, *Rolling Dice*, *Out of Tune*, *The Beach House*, and *The Kissing Booth 2: Going the Distance*.

Alongside writing exciting new fiction novels, Beth blogs regularly about writing and being a twenty-something. She has been shortlisted for the Women of the Future Young Star Award 2013, the Romantic Novel of the Year Awards 2014 and the Queen of Teen Awards 2014. She was named one of *Time* magazine's 16 Most Influential Teenagers 2013, and in August 2014 she was listed in *The Times* at No. 6 on their 'Top 20 under 25' list.

Also by Beth Reekles
The Kissing Booth
Going the Distance
Rolling Dice
Out of Tune

Chapter 1

Every summer since I could remember, we'd head up the coast to the Flynns' beach house. Summer there was like a dream.

Packing for the beach house, though, was always my own personal nightmare.

Always.

It never used to be so bad when my mom did it for me – back when I was a little girl who didn't really know or care what I needed. But now, I would make more of an effort . . . And then lose my patience, upturn my suitcase and start again.

It was mid-morning on Wednesday, the day before we left, and Dad came into my room with a glass of soda for me.

'It looks like a bomb's gone off in here,' he said, laughing.

'I *hate* packing.'

'Don't forget to take aftersun.'

'Okay, okay, okay!' No way was I going to forget that; last year I'd burnt the back of my legs so badly, it had been painful to sit down. My dad looked around the room, shook his head and abandoned me to the chaos.

In the end, I packed the same as always: plenty of swimwear and flip-flops and sun hats, and some shorts and T-shirts. I eventually threw in a yellow sundress that the girls had convinced me to buy on a day out shopping – just in case.

Part of the reason I was having even more trouble packing this year was because I had a boyfriend now, and he'd be there with us. I'd known Noah and Lee Flynn all my life and Lee was my best friend, but in the last few months, Noah had gone from being just Lee's older brother to . . . well, my boyfriend.

Which meant that we might end up going on a date, especially since we weren't sneaking around any more . . .

I smiled at that. No more sneaking around! No more hiding it from my best friend because I was worried we would hurt his feelings. We were *officially* dating.

As much as it made me smile, it also made me want to yank at my hair in frustration. What if I wanted to dress nicer to go out places with Noah? Would there be some kind of new rule that meant I couldn't slouch around in threadbare pajama shorts and a shapeless tank top anywhere near him?

I picked up the pajamas I'd happily worn for the past few months. Definitely not the kind you want your boyfriend to see you in . . . Especially when he's easily the hottest guy in school, with that swoon-worthy smirk . . . but it's not like I had anything different to wear.

I sighed and said to myself, 'To hell with it,' and threw them in my case.

A voice sounded behind me. 'To hell with what?'

'Hi, Lee,' I greeted him, not even having to glance over my shoulder to know my best friend since forever was standing in my doorway.

'What did you do in here – blow up your closet?'

'Yeah. We had a fight. I think it wants to file for divorce.'

He laughed, and I heard him dropping clothes on to the floor from my bed. I turned round to tell him to be careful and not crease my stuff, when he dropped face first on to my duvet.

'What were you grumbling to yourself about?' he asked.

'Nothing, just . . .'

He raised an eyebrow, giving me that unconvinced expression that told me he knew exactly what was up

3

but just wanted to hear me say it. 'Bikini not skimpy enough for my brother?'

I threw a tank top at him. 'No, it's not that.'

'Then what? Oh, man, no, don't tell me you're gonna make me go shopping for lingerie or something? Please, Shelly, anything but that! Tampons, I can do, but not – *not* – lingerie!'

I laughed. Lee was about the only person I'd let get away with calling me 'Shelly' instead of 'Elle' (short for Rochelle), although Noah would use the nickname too, just to tease me. 'Not that either. It's my pajamas.'

'Oh, that's all you're worried about?' Lee laughed. He rolled on my bed and leaned over the edge to look into my case. 'You'll look fine whatever you're wearing. Besides, it's not like he's really going to care.'

I smiled at Lee. No matter what it was that was getting me down, he could always brighten me back up in an instant.

'How long have you been packing now anyway?' he asked. 'Eighteen hours?'

I wavered. 'Eight.'

My best friend gave me a long, flat look, and then we both burst out laughing.

'I'm going to take a wild guess and say that *you* –' I pointed an accusing finger at him – 'haven't even started packing yet.'

'*You*,' he told me, pointing a finger back at me, 'would be totally right.'

Lee cleared his throat suddenly and picked up my pillow, tweaking at the pillowcase.

'So . . . you're still cool Rachel's coming with us, right?'

You've only asked about a billion times . . .

It was like he was worried I'd throw a tantrum, tell him he couldn't change things this year and how dare he bring his girlfriend!

I mean, in a way, yeah, I wanted to tell him that I didn't want Rachel there. I wanted it to be the same as it always was and always had been.

But how selfish would that be?

For one thing, I was dating his older brother. I could hardly tell Lee I didn't want him to bring his girlfriend along when I'd have *my* boyfriend there.

Besides, even if I wasn't with Noah, things were always going to be different this year anyway.

Noah wouldn't be staying the whole time: he was leaving two days earlier than the rest of us with his dad to check out the Harvard campus. They were flying to Massachusetts while we stayed behind.

I hated that things had to change. Growing up, I'd thought we'd always have the beach house. That no matter what, every summer we'd go there – and for just

5

a couple of days, we could act like kids and just hang out. Even when we'd gotten older, and Noah drifted away from us to go to parties on the beach in the night or make out with random girls who fawned over him, he'd always come back to hang out with us. Because there, with the sea and the sand and nobody else around, none of us cared what anybody thought. Summer at the beach house meant everything was different, but different in the best kind of way.

Except this year, I wasn't so sure.

I blinked, looking at Lee and pulling myself out of my thoughts.

It didn't matter if I was cool with Rachel coming with us or not – she was Lee's girlfriend. I had to be okay with it, for him.

It was lucky I liked her.

'Yeah, of course I am,' I answered him. 'When did you say she's coming down?'

'Monday,' he told me. 'And her family is picking her up on Thursday afternoon, on their way to visit some relatives.'

'Okay.' I nodded and grabbed a pair of pants from the floor, folding them up.

'Elle, are you sure you're okay about –'

'Yes!' I laughed to reinforce my words. 'Yes, I'm okay about it, Lee, for the billionth time already! Besides, it'll be nice for your mom and me to have some female company for a change. There's only so much of you we can handle, you know.'

'I did catch on to that,' he said with a smirk. 'Given how little time we've spent together over the past few years.'

Both of us laughed, and I grinned at Lee.

'Go on, get your butt back home and start packing!' I shoved him off my bed. 'If you forget to pack your trunks again this year, you are not borrowing one of my bikinis. I do not need a repeat performance of *that*!'

Six thirty the next morning, I was at the top of the staircase, ready to haul my suitcase down to the porch. A knock sounded on the front door and Lee opened it, stepping inside.

'Whoa, watch it!' he exclaimed, and was suddenly leaping up the stairs to take my bag from me before I got past the third step. I'd been gripping the banister hard to keep myself from toppling over – my suitcase weighed a ton.

'Thanks,' I said.

As we reached the door, there was movement from near the kitchen. Lee looked past me and I turned to see my dad standing there in his pajamas and old burgundy robe, his glasses sitting a little crooked on his face and too far down his nose. He pushed them back up.

'You kids ready to set off, then?'

'Yup,' the two of us answered in unison.

'You know the drill: no mad parties drinking tequila, don't swim out too far, be nice to the other kids . . .'

'We know,' we chorused.

Dad laughed, but it broke off with a yawn. 'I know, I know, same parental spiel as every year, right? Come on then, Elle, let's have a hug before you go.'

I went over and gave my dad a hug and a kiss on the cheek.

'Be careful.'

I rolled my eyes. What did he think I was going to do – see if I could beat up a shark and live to tell the tale? Honestly . . .

'You know what I mean, Elle.'

I frowned questioningly at him. Did I?

Lee coughed pointedly by the door, and Dad shifted from foot to foot and crossed his arms. He clenched his jaw briefly, looking uncomfortable, then said, 'With Noah.'

Somehow, I managed to keep my cheeks from flaming. Instead, I sighed and rolled my eyes again elaborately.

On the bright side, at least Lee didn't make any sarcastic comments. It was bad enough that he'd bought me a pack of condoms for my birthday. Then he'd given them to me in front of not only his parents and Noah, and my ten-year-old brother, but my dad too! Lee's way of dealing with the awkwardness of me dating his brother was to crack jokes.

You can just imagine how much the whole condoms thing had made me laugh. Ha-ha.

'I'll be fine, Dad, stop worrying. I'll call you when we get there,' I said.

'All right, bud.' He smiled and, for a second, he looked more like a forty-seven-year-old man than he usually did. But only for a moment, and by then I'd already started back to the front door. Lee picked up my suitcase before I had the chance to.

'Lee?'

He half-turned toward to my dad. 'Yeah?'

'Look after my little girl for me, will you?'

It wasn't Dad I was looking at now, it was my best friend. And he was looking back at me with a soft, friendly smile on his face. His blue eyes were warm and familiar, and the freckles spattered across his nose were embedded in my memory, as they had been for over a decade. I felt the sudden urge to hug him tight and be glad that whatever else went on, however much things changed with us getting boyfriends and girlfriends and growing up, I always had Lee.

A small part of me, in a voice that sounded oddly like Lee's in my mind, told me to stop being so cheesy.

'Don't worry,' Lee said, watching me, and I could tell his thoughts were on the same wavelength as mine. 'I will.'

Chapter 2

The journey went by way more quickly than usual. Instead of all cramming into his dad's car, this year Lee and I were in Lee's '65 convertible Mustang and the two of us spent the whole drive singing along to the radio at the top of our lungs and joking around.

Well, that – or Lee was speeding.

We arrived after the others, though they couldn't have been there for very long; Matthew, Lee's dad, was only just shutting the trunk and locking the car. He gave us a smile and a wave.

'Roads okay?'

I swung out of the car, and put my huge straw bag up on to my shoulder. 'Yeah.'

Lee was still in the driver's seat, clearing up the jumble of candy-bar wrappers and empty drink bottles. He was so normally messy, but way too proud of his car to leave trash in there.

I opened up the trunk and tried to get a good grip on my suitcase. I started to hoist it out, and wondered what the hell I'd packed for the next ten days that made it so heavy.

'Need to borrow some muscle?'

I let go of my bag with a surprised huff and it slid back into the car with a heavy *thunk*. I twisted my head to look over my shoulder, hair falling in my face, to see Noah, as sexy and handsome as ever, arching a dark eyebrow with his trademark smug look on his face.

My heart somersaulted in my chest and I couldn't hold back my smile – even if I'd only just seen him two days ago. Noah grinned as I stepped toward him for a kiss, his arms wrapping round my waist to hold me closer. He smelled so *good*. And looked it, too, in his board shorts and a fitted white T-shirt.

'Hey, you.'

'Hey, yourself,' he murmured, his mouth smiling against mine. 'So – want a hand with your bag?'

'It's all yours, Superman.'

I couldn't resist making that dig – just before we got together, I'd caught him wearing Superman boxers. And he'd actually been embarrassed about it! Noah Flynn, the school badass, the jerk who I always argued with . . . wearing Superman boxers.

He hated it whenever I brought it up. But teasing him was irresistible sometimes.

He dropped a kiss on my cheek before lugging my suitcase out of the trunk and following me up the steps of the porch. The white paint of it was always flaking, no matter how many times Lee's parents gave us twenty bucks to spend an afternoon painting it again. The bench on the porch creaked like it was about to snap in half every time you sat down; I ran a hand over the arm of it as I passed to go inside.

The beach house had a lot of rooms, but they were all small, packed tightly together. The furniture hadn't been replaced in years, some of it from when we were little kids. There was a pool outside and a table we usually ate at in the evenings if it wasn't raining, and a path that was always overgrown with rough plants leading down to the beach. The whole thing was the polar opposite of the immaculately put-together Flynn home in the city and its modern decor.

We loved it exactly as it was – a little shabby, lived-in and worn, and homey.

In my eyes, it was perfect.

'I'm just going to run and get some food,' June announced, walking out of the kitchen as I was coming down the hallway. She smiled when she saw me. 'Hey, Elle, sweetie.'

I said hello and hugged her while Noah squeezed past to drop my suitcase in my room.

'Do you want some company to the store?' I offered.

'No, no, that's okay. You stay here and unpack.'

Then, holding me at a little distance and looking at me with that gentle, motherly smile she always wore, June said something that caught me totally off guard, because it was so out of the blue.

'Look at you, Elle. You suddenly seem so grown-up.'

'Why? Because I had to use that special zipper that makes my suitcase expand?'

'No.' She laughed. 'I don't know – I can't quite pinpoint it. You just seem like you've become a real young woman recently. Anyway – listen to me rambling on like this! I'm getting out of here before I find myself looking for any baby photos lying around! Oh, and tell the boys we're having steak for dinner.'

'Sure thing,' I called as June headed back toward the kitchen.

I started down the hallway in the direction of the bedrooms. Lee and I had ours side by side with Noah's, separated by a bathroom in the middle that we all shared. It might've made more sense for the boys to have a room together, but they'd always bickered so much when we were little, it had been Lee and me who'd shared – and we'd just never changed that. (And despite how cool June and Matthew were, they'd made a point of drawing the line at me sharing a room with Noah.)

Noah was on his way back outside, and stopped in the kitchen doorway.

'Thanks for the help with my suitcase.'

'What, that's it? I don't get a tip?'

I laughed, as if to tell him, *No chance*. He caught my wrist and stepped in front of me in the doorframe to pin me there.

'Hey, I'm an awesome bellboy and you know it,' he said, his voice just as serious as his expression.

I bit back a laugh, but a grin spread over my face. 'You tell yourself that.' I went up on my toes to give him a peck on the lips. Instead of letting me pull away, though, Noah drew me in for a soft, sweet kiss, more intimate than the one we'd just shared outside. His fingers dropped from round my wrist to link themselves through my fingers.

A throat cleared – we both jumped.

I turned my head ready to stare meaningfully at Lee, make a comment about how I'd interrupt him every time he kissed Rachel once she got here; but the opportunity never came and the words stuck in my throat.

'Can I get through?' Matthew said. Noah stepped back and tugged me round the doorframe to let his dad through. I was so mortified that for a moment all I could do was bite my tongue and make a mental note to never, ever kiss in a doorway ever again.

I was jerked out of my thoughts when I felt a gentle tug on my ponytail. Noah chuckled. 'Shelly, anyone would think you're not *used* to being seen with your boyfriend.'

'Anyone would think we dated in secret for months,' I deadpanned, rolling my eyes, still embarrassed. 'Are you sure your parents don't mind me coming this year?'

I sounded like Lee, asking yet again if it was cool that Rachel was coming for a few days. I searched Noah's face for a hint that maybe his parents had said something to him they wouldn't say to me, that maybe they'd had some debate about whether or not I should come along this year, after all the drama I'd caused.

Noah squeezed my hand, which had suddenly turned clammy, and his touch seemed to undo all the knots in my stomach. 'Totally sure. Hey, why don't you go unpack? I told my dad I'd clean up outside.'

I let him kiss me again, feeling a little better as we parted, and I went into my room, where Lee was already stuffing clothes into his drawer of the dresser. He smiled at me and I relaxed further. Of course

Matthew and June wanted me here. If they didn't, Lee would have told me. He wouldn't be able to hide something like that.

'Maybe I shouldn't have brought so much stuff,' I panted, after hauling my bag from the floor on to the bed to sort through it.

'That might just about be the smartest thing you've said yet, Elle.'

'Ha-ha.'

'See,' Lee said, 'if this was last summer, I'd be making a joke about how you have an excuse to see my brother flex his muscles and actually *talk* to him, since you're so in love with him, except . . . Well, you *are* in love with him. So it kind of loses all effect.'

I laughed. 'It's still funny, Lee, don't worry.'

'Yeah, but that's because I am a comedian *extraordinaire*.' He laughed. 'It's not the same, though.'

I sighed, suddenly annoyed. 'What do you want me to say? Sorry?'

Lee frowned. 'I didn't mean it like that, Shelly.'

He turned away, shoving one last T-shirt into the drawer. Something crackled in the air between us – something I still wasn't used to. A tension we liked to ignore because Lee was still hurt by the fact I'd lied to him for so long, and had made him feel like I'd picked Noah over him somehow.

'I didn't mean it like that,' he told me again, more softly this time.

'I know.'

Lee sucked in a sharp breath and grinned at me to diffuse the mood. 'Now, hurry up, find your bikini, and go change. I want to get down to the beach already.'

Living in California, the past few weeks at home had been sun, sun, sun – but there was something special about the beach. Summer just seemed a lot brighter when we were only minutes away from the sea.

Twenty minutes later, Lee and I were making our way down the beaten sandy track between the shrubbery and on to the beach, ignoring Noah's shout when we passed that we could help him tidy up a little. I spread my towel out carefully before flopping down on to it, putting in my earphones and finding a playlist on my phone. I put on the red plastic five-dollars-from-a-gas-station sunglasses I'd made Lee stop to buy on the way here. I still couldn't believe I'd forgotten mine.

I heard Lee clear his throat loudly, and I twisted my head up to look at him.

Pushing his Ray-Bans into his hair, messing it up, he said, 'What are you doing?'

'Um . . . sunbathing?'

He sighed irritably, frowning. Then he actually wagged a finger at me, like I was a misbehaving puppy. 'You're such a *girl*, sometimes, Rochelle Evans.'

I raised my eyebrows at him briefly, especially after he'd used my full name, then looked down at myself. I dropped my jaw melodramatically. 'What do you know? I *am* a girl!'

He laughed and kicked some sand over my legs. 'You know what I mean. Let's go get the bodyboards already.'

'Tell you what. You go get the bodyboards, and I will stay here soaking up some sunshine.'

'Um, let me think about that . . . ah – *no*.'

'Yes!'

'Fine. But I won't be held responsible for which board you end up with.'

Before I could say anything, he'd taken off, spraying sand behind him. I sighed and shook my head, settling down on my towel and wriggling around a little to get comfortable.

Something poked my leg, and a voice said, 'Hey, lazy.'

'Can't I have, like, two seconds of peace?' I joked, sitting up and pulling off my glasses so Noah would know I was mock-glaring at him. He just chuckled, throwing his towel in a heap next to me.

I put my glasses back on and couldn't help it when my gaze accidentally caught Noah's abs. It occurred to me how weird it was that in all the years we'd been coming here, I'd never used it as an excuse to check Noah out. I mean, I guess I'd been having too much fun or joking around to really pay attention to Noah. And then, when I did have a crush on him, when I was, like, twelve, I'd gone through a stage of barely being able to talk around him, let alone bring myself to see if he had abs when he was thirteen or fourteen.

I shook myself, and glanced up to see if he'd caught me ogling him. I just knew he'd have that sexy smirk on his face that made me blush for no real reason – and I did blush, but not because he was smirking; he was checking *me* out.

I pushed my glasses up again, and his eyes snapped back to my face. This time, it was my turn to smirk.

He said innocently, 'What, I can't appreciate how gorgeous my girlfriend is?'

I laughed. 'If only I could appreciate how cheesy my boyfriend is.'

'Aw, come on. You love the cheesy stuff.'

My smile turned sheepish. 'Kinda.'

He chuckled again, and offered me his hand. I took it, letting him help me to my feet. Noah pulled me into his arms and planted a kiss on my forehead. I started to lift my head so I could kiss him properly when –

'Ew, cooties.'

'Lee . . .' I complained, turning slightly in Noah's arms. I rolled my eyes at him, but my best friend just gave an impish grin, and he swung round the bodyboards he was holding.

He tossed a black one with a white logo to Noah, kept a blue bodyboard in his own hand, and then tossed me a bright pink one. I fumbled to catch it before it hit me in the face, and then I saw the big 'Barbie' logo on it, and all the pink flowers and hearts.

'Lee!'

'What? I told you, I wouldn't be held responsible for –'

'Yeah, yeah,' I muttered, but I was smiling. 'Come on, then. Let's get this party started.'

Lee sighed and clapped a hand on my shoulder, and Noah's laugh turned into a cough.

'Shelly . . . please, promise me one thing,' Lee said.

'What?'

'Never say that again.'

Chapter 3

I stood in front of the mirror, scrutinizing my outfit of shorts and a tank top. Lee was chattering away at me, but I found myself not really listening. Lee noticed and paused, tilting his head. 'What's up?'

I just bit my lip, suddenly nervous. I could feel my heart thudding hard against my ribcage and I gulped.

I knew things couldn't be completely the same this year, sure. I knew that things might even be a little weird now that Noah and I were a couple and not just hanging out any more. But it had only just hit me. The realization that this felt like dinner with their parents as *Noah's girlfriend*, not as Lee's best friend.

'Shelly.'

'It's nothing,' I answered. 'It's fine. I'm fine.'

But really?

Yeah, I was kind of freaking out inside. What if things were *really* weird? What if things were awkward now? Should I be trying to make a better impression?

As Noah's girlfriend, should I be dressing up a little? What if – what if – what if –

Lee's stomach growled.

'Shelly, are you coming or what?'

Do I have a choice?

'Sure. Sorry.' I forced a smile out for him, but I knew he didn't believe it for a second.

We went outside, where Noah and his parents were just sitting down. Plates were loaded with food, I was half expecting the table to collapse under the weight of it all.

'I hope you kids are hungry,' June said.

Lee's stomach growled again in answer to his mom, and we all laughed. Lee and I sat down in our usual seats. And, of course, my usual seat was in the middle of Noah and Lee – so they wouldn't fight at the table, June had always said. I'd never had a problem with it, even when they were arguing across me.

Never had a problem with it up until now, anyway. Because now, I felt kind of claustrophobic sitting between my best friend and my boyfriend.

If anyone else felt as irrationally paranoid as I did, they didn't show it. The boys were stuffing their faces on either side of me, and June and Matthew were discussing plans to visit an art gallery tomorrow. Noah must have noticed something was up, though, because he nudged his knee against mine, catching my eye to give me a reassuring smile. I breathed a small sigh of relief, wanting to laugh at myself for being such a complete idiot, and dug into my food.

Once I did, the atmosphere was just as relaxed as it always had been, and I was glad that at least something went unchanged this year. Soon enough, I'd forgotten why I'd even been so worried in the first place.

'So, Rachel's getting here at –'

'Don't talk with your mouth full, Lee.'

He swallowed hard. 'So Rachel's getting here at one o'clock on Monday.'

'We know,' Noah said irritably. 'You haven't shut up about it since Mom said she could come down for a few days.'

'That's because he's in *love*,' I said teasingly, bumping my shoulder into Lee's and grinning at him.

'Have you kids got anything planned for tomorrow, then?' Matthew asked us, and I got the feeling he was trying to hastily change the subject.

'Beach,' Lee said.

'Sunbathing,' I said. Then I added, 'And Noah's going to stomp around the beach destroying kids' sandcastles again . . .'

'What?' June exclaimed, like she wasn't sure whether to be shocked or to laugh.

'That,' Noah said, poking me in the ribs, 'was an accident.'

I gave him a skeptical look, trying to keep my face straight. 'Sure.'

'I did *not* do it on purpose,' he said, enunciating every word. 'Besides, he shouldn't have been building a sandcastle with a giant moat round it anyway.'

'He fell in the moat,' Lee told his parents, snickering at the memory of Noah face-planting into the poor kid's sandcastle and completely wrecking all the kid's hard work.

'But when you were gonna help him build it back up?' I said, a grin slipping on to my face. 'That was cute. Really *cute*.'

I had a flashback of Noah trying to mash handfuls of damp sand together to pacify the little kid whose sandcastle he'd just flattened. The boy had thrown a tantrum and run off to get his mommy. Noah ran in the opposite direction back to us while we howled with laughter at the sight of Noah Flynn, school badass, running scared. Lee had pointed out that six-year-olds with an angry mom in tow are pretty damn scary, which I didn't argue with.

But still. It was cute that he'd tried to fix the sandcastle.

'I'm sorry,' Noah said. 'What was it?'

'Absolutely insanely *cute*.'

'Right, that's it!'

Next thing I knew, Noah had shot out of his seat and grabbed me round the waist, tossing me over his shoulder. I shouted, but I was laughing too hard to wriggle out of his grip. He started marching away from the table.

I suddenly got a sinking feeling in my gut. He couldn't be walking toward the pool, right? He'd walk round it. He wouldn't –

My body hit the water with a sharp *slap*. I shot to the surface again and bobbed there, my clothes billowing out around me. My teeth immediately started chattering a little too. I never knew the water was so cold at night!

I could hear everyone laughing from the table outside the kitchen. Noah was silhouetted against the house with his arms folded, and I could just about make out the giant smirk on his face.

'I'm going to kill you for this, Noah Flynn!' I called up to him as I waded over to the edge of the pool. 'Now I have to go wash my hair all over again and –'

Noah crouched down as I reached the edge and interrupted me, saying, 'You're hot when you're angry.'

I looked at him for a long moment before splashing him in the face.

He chuckled quietly. It was too dark to tell whether he could see or not, but I rolled my eyes at him all the same.

'Give me a hand?' I asked, reaching up to him. Underwater, I braced my feet against the wall of the pool.

He started to say something, but cut himself off, and took my hand to heave me up. Immediately, I started tugging down to try and make him fall in the water. I knew he'd probably guess what I was up to, but I thought maybe I'd pull it off – and pull him in the pool.

As it turned out, Noah was a hell of a lot stronger than I gave him credit for. He didn't even wobble off balance. He just stood up, dragging me out of the water so I hung from his hand like a fish on a rod.

'I have to say, Elle, I didn't think you were that predictable.'

'It's all part of my master plan.'

Noah set me down on the tiles that surrounded the pool – and as soon as he let me go, Lee was barreling toward him, tackling him and sending them both into the water, drenching me again with the splash they caused. June burst into laughter but still called, 'Boys! Be careful!'

Lee surfaced, shaking the water off his head like a dog and beaming at me. 'See, Shelly? I've always got your back.'

I blew him a kiss. 'My knight in shining armor.'

Noah grabbed Lee's legs from under the water and I caught the brief look of horror on Lee's face before he was dunked, sending me into helpless giggles.

Later that evening, after I'd washed the chlorine out of my hair, there was a light knock on the bedroom door.

'Uh . . . come in?'

I was a little surprised to find it was June. 'Hi, Elle.'

'Hey. Everything okay?'

'Oh, yeah. I just thought – well, I thought maybe we could have a little chat. Girl to girl.' She took a seat on the end of Lee's bed, looking unusually serious.

'Okay . . .'

So I was right to be worried before dinner, and earlier today. Things had changed. Whatever June wanted to talk about, I had the sinking feeling it was to do with me and Noah.

'Elle . . . Look, honey, I'm only asking you this because I care about you. I'm not going out of my way to make you feel awkward.' She smiled reassuringly. 'I'm just a little confused about you and Noah is all. What you're going to do when he goes to college, I mean.'

'Oh!' That was all? 'Oh, well, we were just going to . . . you know, make the most of summer. And it's not like he'll never be home from college. And we can video chat. We'll make it work.'

I trailed off at the look June was giving me.

It was the kind of look people like parents and teachers give you that says, *Oh, you're so young, you just don't know.* It wasn't the kind of look I was used to getting from June, and I bristled.

'Really? You think that's the best option?' She spoke kindly, not in a condescending way, which was some comfort.

'W-well – I mean, yeah ... It's ... Long-distance relationships can work out. And I know we've only been together a few months, but it's different for Noah and me. We've always known each other.'

'Do you remember when you were really little? And you used to dress up as a princess and say when you grew up you'd live in a castle with your Prince Charming?'

I buried my face in my hands for a second, laughing in embarrassment. 'Oh, gosh, I'd forgotten about that.'

'Honey, I'm a mom. It's my job to remind you all about the embarrassing things you did when you were a kid.'

I laughed again, and sat on the end of my bed so I was facing June. She put a hand on my knee.

'Don't get me wrong, Elle. I've seen the way you two look at each other. I know you're both in love. But right now, it's easy. When Noah leaves for college, it's going to take a lot more work. I want you both to go into that with your eyes open.'

'Have you had this talk with Noah as well?' I couldn't help asking.

She nodded. 'I'm not trying to be the bad guy here and say it won't work out, or that you shouldn't try. That's not what I'm doing. I'd just hate to see you both get hurt. I want to make sure you've both really thought about this. Relationships aren't like the fairy tales, Elle. It takes work.'

I didn't know what to say. I knew she wanted a different answer than the one I was going to give her.

'Just a mom's perspective on things,' she said, holding her hands up in defense. Then she pushed herself up off the bed. 'I'll let you get some rest. You're probably asleep on your feet.'

I managed a smile. She was right; another few minutes and I'd be sleeping sitting up. It had been a long day.

I said goodnight to June and sat still for a moment, staring at the closed door. There were scratches on the faded wood, where Lee and I had measured each other every year we'd come here. I stared at the notches blankly, a jumble of thoughts running through my head.

It was going to work out for me and Noah, right? A long-distance relationship?

There *would* be a hell of a distance between us, plus a couple of hours' time difference. And being with Noah had almost cost me Lee's friendship. It hadn't exactly been easy to get to this point.

But I didn't want to lose Noah. I didn't want us to break up. I wanted a long-distance relationship and for us to make it work.

Did he feel the same way, though?

June's apprehension clung to me. I wondered if, despite having the best intentions, she'd made Noah doubt all of this too.

Because what if he didn't want to give it a shot now? What if –

'Knock, knock?'

Lee. I got up, opening the door. He smiled that easy smile of his, holding a steaming mug in each hand. 'What's going on? What's wrong?'

I took the mug he handed to me. 'Hot chocolate in the middle of summer?'

'Of course!' he said, grinning. He sat down on his bed facing me, where his mom had been only minutes before. 'Mom said you looked like you needed it. What's up?'

'Nothing's up, it's –'

He groaned. 'What's my mom said to you now?'

'Nothing! Well, I mean, no, she was saying . . . She didn't say it in so many words, but she obviously thinks me and Noah shouldn't try staying together when he goes to college and I just . . . I don't know! Does he even want to stay with me? He's never had a long-term relationship, *ever*. He probably wants to break up at the end of summer so he can find some really hot, really smart girl who he actually sees and who doesn't live all the way across the country, you know. It's like –'

'Whoa, okay, hold it right there, or you're going to lose me,' Lee interrupted. I gave a small laugh and sipped at my hot chocolate. 'First off, he won't want to break up with you. End of conversation.'

I laughed again. 'You're really, really helpful sometimes, you know that?'

'I do know that.'

I shook my head. 'You know what, it doesn't even matter. Forget I said anything.'

Lee looked ready to push it, to *really* talk to me. And he was my best friend. I could talk to him about anything.

But not this.

This wasn't a conversation I had to have with Lee. It was one I had to have with Noah.

So, before he could open his mouth, I said, 'What's going on when Rachel gets here, anyway? Where's she sleeping?'

'My bed,' Lee told me. 'I'm camping out on the floor in Noah's room for a couple of nights.'

'Oh, right. Okay then.'

'You don't mind, do you? Sharing a room with Rachel, I mean? You're okay with it?'

I looked at him over the top of my mug and smiled. Even if I'd hated Rachel's guts (which was totally impossible as she was really nice), I'd have put up with her for Lee. 'Of course I don't mind, Lee. Seriously. It's going to be totally fine.'

. . . Wasn't it?

Chapter 4

The next couple of days passed before I could blink. We'd get up late, go to the beach and bodyboard or swim, maybe play some Frisbee, have some lunch, and then either head back to the beach or stay around our little pool for the afternoon.

And Noah and I managed to steal a few moments alone together. Although, the one time we thought we finally had the house to ourselves, his parents had come home early. We'd barely managed to grab our clothes from around the pool before they came through the house to say hi.

By Sunday, Lee was getting all pent up. Rachel was arriving the next day and he was like an excited puppy dog. But that also meant he was all over the place. He told us he was going to get ice creams, but came back with a pair of flippers.

I didn't even ask.

Lee was texting Rachel so much, I got totally exasperated with his phone bleeping every four seconds, and eventually snapped, 'For God's sake, Lee, just go call her! Jeez!'

Noah chuckled, but Lee just chirpily said, 'Okay!' and was already dialing her number as he walked off.

'He is so in love, it's almost stopped being funny,' Noah told me gravely. 'How long do you think it'll be until I have to put on a penguin suit for the wedding?'

I laughed. 'Hmm, I say two years.'

'That long? Really?'

'Oh, come on. You know Lee. He'll want to make sure the flowers and the food and the cake are just perfect. And he'll want the perfect bachelor party too.'

'Which, of course, I'd be in charge of planning.'

'You think you'll be his best man?'

'Who else? I'm his big brother. I've got plenty of embarrassing stories about him. I'm the obvious choice.'

'I think you'll find the position of best *wo*man is already taken.'

Noah laughed. 'Of course it is. I'm really thirsty,' he said suddenly. 'Do you want to grab a Coke from the bar?'

A bit further down the shore was a little beach shop, a surf shack and a bar. I loved the bar on the beach;

there was something about it that made me think of the Caribbean. It had a thick straw roof, shaped like a giant parasol, and the drinks were always served with little paper umbrellas in them.

'Sure,' I answered.

He dug underneath his towel for his wallet, taking out a few dollar bills. 'Let's go.'

It didn't take long to get there, but the queue looked like it would take a while for us to be served. I was glancing around and caught sight of a few guys talking. They were looking at Noah. He had his back to them, so he didn't see, but I got the sinking feeling they were talking about him.

'Do you know those guys? Over there?' I blurted out. Knowing me, I could've just been overreacting and they weren't even looking at him.

Noah looked round, right at the guys who were staring at him. I guessed they were maybe around our age – soon-to-be-seniors or freshmen at college.

I was about to grab Noah's arm, thinking that it was stupid for him to look at them so obviously, but then I realized that he most likely didn't give a damn if he annoyed them or not. He turned back, not looking fazed at all, and before I could say another word the barman got to us.

'What can I get you guys?'

'Two Cokes,' Noah said, pushing the money across the counter. He looked over at the guys again, scowling at them this time.

'Noah!' I exclaimed, swatting his hand when he didn't reply. 'Do you know them or what?' I sent another fleeting glance at them and said, 'They're still looking over here.'

'Yeah, if it's the guy I think it is, I made out with his ex-girlfriend or something last summer. He tried to punch me so, naturally, I acted in self-defense. Might not even be him,' he said flippantly.

'What? When did –'

'You know all those beach bonfires and parties and stuff? You and Lee never went to them?' I nodded. Noah jerked a thumb over his shoulder in the general direction of the boys looking at him. 'I think it was at one of those.'

'I can't believe . . .' I trailed off and shook my head. 'You couldn't have just walked away?'

Noah ground his teeth and hung his head. 'Point taken.'

The barman set down two tall glasses of Coke in front of us. I mumbled thanks and took a sip of mine.

We picked up the conversation I'd interrupted earlier, talking easily until we finished our drinks. But I couldn't help it – I kept glancing past Noah, my eyes flickering over to the boys who'd looked at him before. One had a sneer on his face and the other two were laughing. It gave me a queasy kind of feeling in my stomach.

I was still taken by surprise, though, when we got up to leave and someone suddenly slammed into Noah. It was completely on purpose, but the guy – the blond guy who'd been sneering – backed off, saying in a sarcastic tone, 'Whoa, sorry, dude. Didn't even see you there.'

I saw the muscle in Noah's jaw jumping.

He shoved the blond guy back – not even hard; it was like a poke more than a shove. 'Why don't you watch where you're going, huh?'

The guy scoffed, and his two friends had stupid grins on their faces too. 'Right, right, sure.'

Noah's fingers were curling into fists at his side, then flexing out again. I grabbed his arm. 'Hey. Come on. Let's just go. They're not worth it, Noah.'

The blond guy looked at me, then sneered at Noah again. 'So, whose girl did you steal this year, Flynn?'

Noah stared scornfully at the blond guy like he would a piece of dirt on his precious motorbike. 'Get over yourself.'

He started to walk off, and I was totally shocked for a moment; Noah Flynn, the most badass guy in the entire school, walking away from a fight?

Wow. Maybe he really had changed.

But the blond dude and his friends weren't having it; the blond guy deliberately stepped into Noah's path, shoving him again. I looked around, wondering where the hell Lee was when I needed him.

'Come on, now,' Noah said. 'You really want to pick a fight in front of a lady?'

The blond guy made as if to shove Noah again to make his point, but Noah sidestepped and the guy lost his balance and went sprawling on his front, spitting sand from his mouth.

Before he got back up, or his friends decided to cause more trouble, I took Noah's hand. 'Let's get out of here.'

He nodded, following me down the beach.

I looked back a couple of times, and the blond guy was shaking people off him, storming away. Despite not laying a hand on him, it seemed that Noah had damaged his pride a hell of a lot.

'You *think* you might've made out with his ex-girlfriend last year?' I repeated, stumbling over my own feet somewhat before falling into step with Noah.

'All right, all right. But in my defense, they weren't together at the time. If you ask me, he's just an asshole.'

'And you feel the need to pick a fight with every asshole guy you come across? We both know you would've if I hadn't been there.'

Noah tugged me closer, letting go of my hand to wrap his arm round my shoulders. 'You really know how to guilt-trip me, don't you, Elle?'

'I'm serious. I need you to know you can't solve everything by throwing a few punches any more. I don't . . . I don't want you getting in trouble at Harvard.'

'I do know. I get it, okay? My parents have been going on and on and on about it all summer too. No more fighting. No more being stupid or reckless or any of that. I know. I'm working on it.'

I was too surprised to say anything else for a moment. Noah sounded weirdly determined. He gave me an awkward smile, looking embarrassed. I'd never thought too much about what his parents might have said to him on the subject of getting into fights. This was the first I'd heard about it from Noah.

'Well, whatever they said, it's obviously made an impression. The old Noah would've punched that guy, *and* his friends. And I totally would've yelled at you for it, for the record.'

'Oh, I know.'

We'd made it back to our spot on the beach by then. Lee was still nowhere to be seen. I settled back down on my towel.

'Hey, Elle?'

'Yeah?'

'I'm trying. To be a better guy. To not be so impulsive. I . . . I want you to know that.'

'I know. I just – I hope you're not doing it for me. You know? Or not *just* for me.'

'I'm not. Although you are a big factor.' His tone had turned teasing now, and I raised my eyebrows. 'Couldn't have you being mad at me, Elle.'

'Make sure you remember that if there's a next time.'

'I'm going swimming; you coming?'

'No,' I said lazily. 'I'm gonna stay here. Finish listening to my podcast.'

Noah nodded, bending to give me a kiss before he strode down to the sea. I watched him go, thinking again how he'd avoided a fight at the bar. I guessed he really was changing.

Chapter 5

On Monday morning, I woke up at what felt like the crack of dawn after a bad night's sleep.

I groaned, tossing about and tumbling off the bed.

'Sorry,' Lee whispered loudly. 'Did I wake you up?'

'A rampaging bull in a china shop is quieter than you, Lee.' I rubbed my eyes and yawned. 'What're you even doing up already?'

'Rachel's coming today and . . .' He trailed off, since that was explanation enough. While part of me thought it was adorable that Lee was getting up so early to try to tidy things so the room wouldn't be a complete wreck when his girlfriend arrived, I still narrowed my sleepy eyes at him.

'What time is it?'

'Seven.'

That was when I threw my pillow at him.

He laughed and caught it, tossing it back over on to my bed. I shot him another glare for waking me up so early, grabbed my bikini and a pair of shorts, and went into the bathroom. I wasn't going to be able to get back to sleep now, but maybe a shower would wake me up properly.

I checked both doors were shut on either side of the bathroom that we shared; the only lock was on Noah's door, and it had never even worked properly. We had a very simple system – if the doors were shut, the bathroom was occupied.

The bathroom wasn't big anyway, but with Lee's hair products scattered everywhere and my toiletries laid out neatly, plus Noah's few things thrown down anywhere, it seemed pretty small and very cluttered. I shoved Lee's stuff to the edge of a shelf to put my clothes down.

I had just lathered up my hair when I heard a door open. I sighed sharply through my nose and stuck my head round the shower curtain, shampoo trickling down the sides of my face. 'Lee, I don't care what time Rachel's coming, your hair gel can wait till I'm not in the –'

Noah took one look at me and started laughing.

'I so need to take a photo of that,' he chuckled, indicating my annoyed face and lathered-up hair.

'Oh, shut up.'

'What's the matter, grumpy-pants, you don't want me to join you?' He smirked, making a show of starting to take off his T-shirt.

'Noah! Stop it.'

We wanted some time alone together during the trip to the beach house, but it wasn't easy. Sure, his room might be *right there* next to mine, but the walls in this place were thin. And that didn't exactly scream romantic or sexy to me. Not with my best friend and his parents around.

'Stop what?' he asked, undoing his belt now, still grinning at me.

'You are *not* doing a striptease in the bathroom,' I hissed at him, blushing and disappearing back behind the shower curtain to rinse my hair. 'So not fair. Remind me why we thought we could handle not having any time to ourselves here?'

'What's the matter, Elle? Need a cold shower?'

I told him to shut up again, smiling when I heard him laugh. It was maddening to be so close to him all the time and not really be able to ... *do* anything. It wasn't even easy to find somewhere else to go and sneak off to. And after our narrow escape near the pool the other day when his parents came back early, I was not about to risk getting caught again.

When I stepped out of the shower, towel wrapped round me, I found Noah finishing up cleaning his teeth, his hair looking tidier than it had a few minutes before. I knocked my hip into him to budge him out of the way so I could get to my stuff.

Noah just kind of hovered by the side of the sink, though, arms folded lightly over his chest and his eyes on me.

'What?'

He shrugged. 'Just thinking.'

'About what?'

'I love you,' was his simple answer, accompanied by a small, genuine smile.

He leaned over the sink to give me a quick kiss on the lips, only a light, little one. He made to leave, but I tugged on his T-shirt to pull him back.

'Hey, you don't get away that easy, mister.' And I kissed him full on the mouth, a smile forming on my face. His arms curled round my waist and he squeezed me closer to him. God, he smelled so good. Had he always smelled this good? I dragged my fingers through his hair, probably messing it back up again.

'Okay. I'm definitely going this time,' he said, drawing away and giving me one last peck on the lips, 'before *I'm* the one who needs a cold shower.'

It turned out Rachel was arriving a few hours earlier than we'd expected, so Lee left to pick her up from the bus station. The beach house wasn't really built for an

45

extra person, but we'd make do having Rachel here too. Lee had an old airbed set up in Noah's room he'd be sleeping on.

I was cuddled up on the sofa with Noah, the two of us watching TV with his parents, when we heard Lee's car pull up outside.

'Sounds like the other pair of lovebirds are here,' June said, she and Matthew getting up to go and greet them. I listened to their conversation for a few minutes, Lee taking Rachel's bag through to the bedroom.

I'd been cool with Rachel coming – but now she was actually here, it felt weird.

I shook myself. I couldn't think like that. It'd be nice having another girl around for a change. And this year, it might be nice to have her here so I didn't feel so guilty about trying to get some time alone with Noah, and not hanging out with Lee.

I looked at the TV, and saw that Noah had switched the channel, settling on some NASCAR program. I watched it for about twenty seconds, then said, 'No way are we watching this. There's got to be something else on. Like cartoons.'

'Cartoons? You're kidding me, right?'

I scowled at Noah, and made to grab the remote from the arm of the couch. He snatched it up and held it above his head.

46

'Noah!' I complained, and scrambled up on the sofa, trying to make a grab – but he kept moving it out of my reach, and I ended up falling across him, almost straddling him, our noses very nearly touching. We looked at each other for a long, long moment; I was biding my time, waiting to lunge for the remote again.

Noah reached up with his free hand to brush some hair behind my ear, and his fingertips lingered near the base of my neck. Then –

I shrieked, falling back on to the sofa and trying to scramble away. Noah was too fast, though, and was lying across me, pinning me down, tickling me ruthlessly. I gasped for air, I was laughing so hard. I tried to wriggle, kick my legs, push his hands away. Nothing worked.

I was wriggling so much that I was right on the edge of the sofa, and Noah let the two of us tumble on to the floor with a loud thud.

'Noah!' I shrieked. 'Noah, stop it!'

He chuckled, grinning mischievously, a devilish gleam in his electric blue eyes. But then his mom called from down the hallway, 'Keep your clothes on!'

We both paused. Sometimes I could see where Lee got it from, when June wasn't above embarrassing us like that. My cheeks were turning red, I could tell, and Noah bit his lip, holding back a laugh. I swatted his chest while my hand was free, because the look on his face was making me want to burst into giggles too. I bit the insides of my cheeks hard.

'Hey, you guys.'

We both looked over to the doorway, where Rachel had stuck her head in. She gave a small wave, which I would've returned if my hands weren't pinned between my chest and Noah's.

'Hey,' we responded.

I said, 'Welcome to the madhouse. Sorry, sorry. Beach house.'

'Rach, come on, my parents want to show you the beach.'

I had never been so glad for Lee's excitable nature as when he wrapped his arms round Rachel's waist and pulled her away, out of the house. I heard the back door rattle closed behind them and, through the windows, saw them all heading down toward the beach.

I turned back to Noah, wiggling one of my hands free to run it through his hair, pushing it away from his face.

He shot me one of his rare smiles then. Not his trademark, sexy smirk, or even half a smile. It was the one that flashed the dimple in his left cheek and was so infectious that I had to smile back at him, getting that warm fuzzy feeling in my stomach.

'So, tomorrow night.'

'Huh?' *Did I miss something?*

'I *was* thinking, we could do something tonight,' he said, 'but we can't because we're all going to this steakhouse, apparently, to welcome Rachel. But we'll do something tomorrow. Just me and you.'

'Did you have anything in particular in mind?'

He tapped his nose. 'I've got a few things up my sleeve.'

'It doesn't involve a monster truck rally, though, right?'

He laughed and tweaked my nose, making me grimace and scrunch up my face. 'No, it doesn't. I know you, Elle. Trust me, you'll love it. If it goes to plan.'

'Goes to plan?'

He shrugged. 'It's a surprise.'

I groaned, frowning at him. 'What's with you and surprises?' I thought for a moment. 'Please tell me you've done something unbearably cute and set up another kissing booth, so we can, like, recreate all the magic of our first kiss.'

Noah laughed again. 'Huh, that *would* have been an idea. Now I'm feeling like you're going to be disappointed it's not that.'

'Can't you just tell me what we're doing if we're going to do something? It sucks not knowing. I feel like an idiot. I won't be disappointed if I know what the surprise is. You can't just tell me? Please?'

He grinned impishly, looking startlingly like Lee for a moment. 'Now where's the fun in that?'

'You just like teasing me like this, don't you?' I pouted.

'Yup, pretty much.' He dipped his head to give me a quick kiss on the lips before jumping to his feet and offering a hand to help me up. I sighed, still pouting at him, but took his hand and stood up too.

'Are you going to watch the rest of the race with me, Elle?' Noah taunted. I looked from him to the car race still going on the TV, and raised my eyebrows as if to say, *You're kidding me*. Noah laughed and sat back down. I sat right down next to him, snuggling up, and even though I really didn't want to watch the race, I was really, really happy.

The others weren't gone long. When they came back, Rachel unpacked a few of her essentials (namely, a swimsuit) and the four of us got ready to head to the beach.

After setting down my towel, I yanked off my T-shirt and stepped out of the shorts I'd put on over my red polka-dot bikini. 'I'm going swimming. Anyone else?'

'Um . . . maybe in ten minutes,' Rachel told me with a bright smile. Her eyes darted over to Lee, and I understood immediately. *Right. Alone time. Gotcha.*

I didn't bother looking at Lee or waiting for him to answer; I turned straight to Noah, who was scrolling through his phone. I pulled on his elbow. 'Come on. Race you.'

He looked at me with a smirk, one dark eyebrow going up. 'Race? What do I get when I win?'

'*If* you win,' I corrected him pointedly. 'Hmm . . .'

'I'm sure I'll think of something,' he told me, winking, with that cocky arrogance I used to wonder why girls swooned over – but which totally worked on me now too. He dropped his phone on his towel, and threw his sunglasses down on top of them.

'Three,' he said, 'two –'

We both took off, kicking up sand, on 'two', like we both knew the other would. I was laughing, a massive smile plastered on my face and the sea breeze tangling my hair as I ran. Feet slipping on the dry, fine sand, it felt so childish, racing him down to the water.

I loved it.

And I loved Noah. But, man, I so wanted to beat him right then.

I was pulling ahead; he was about two steps behind me when I dared to glance back at him. The sand was becoming damper and more solid – I could win this race, easy. My feet were almost at the water's edge now, too . . .

. . . until Noah breezed past and spun to face me from the water, smirking, the sea around his ankles. I stopped in my tracks at the shore, shocked at losing at the very last second.

'No fair.' I pouted.

He laughed provokingly. 'I won fair and square, Shelly,' he said teasingly. 'You owe me.'

I took a couple of steps, the water licking over my feet. 'Ah, but we never agreed on a bet.'

He scoffed, still smirking. 'We both know there's a big, fat IOU with your name signed at the bottom,' he teased. 'Although, we also both knew you were going to lose, so it wasn't really much of a race.'

'I *nearly* won.'

'Sure,' he said, in such a way that I started to wonder if he'd let me pull ahead and think I could win.

I felt a scowl tugging at my forehead, but then I smoothed my expression out to give him a small, flirty smile. I stepped closer until there was only about an inch of space between us, my arms slipping up round his shoulders.

I saw the tiny twitch of his eyebrow going up expectantly, waiting for me to kiss him, and that trademark arrogant smirk of his slipped on to his face again. I went up on my toes, leaning in slowly to kiss him . . .

. . . then shoved him back as hard as I could.

It only worked because I managed to catch him so off guard. It was still like pushing down a brick wall, though – a brick wall with some seriously hot abs, at that. His eyes widened a little and his mouth formed a tiny circle as he toppled back, off balance, caught totally unawares.

He landed with a massive *splash*!

The cold water soaked him completely and I cringed, shrieking a little, as it splattered me wet and cold too.

'That,' I told him, 'is for throwing me in the pool on our first night here.'

Laughing, Noah pushed himself up and shook the water from his hair.

'Sounds fair.' And he pulled me into a kiss, one that sent sparks through me, giving that mind-blowing fireworks feeling.

Chapter 6

I'd been nervous at dinner on my first night – which turned out to have been silly. But on Rachel's first night with us, there was definitely a shift in the atmosphere. I'd panicked that I'd thrown it all off balance by becoming Noah's girlfriend. But it wasn't me who'd made things feel so different: it was Rachel. Tonight, it felt much more like I was going to dinner with everyone as Noah's girlfriend – not as practically part of the family.

Rachel and I were both trying to fit in front of the mirror in the bathroom to do our hair, and our make-up. I put on the yellow sundress I'd bought when I went shopping with Rachel and a couple of the other girls the week before, and threw on some gold jewelry too, at Rachel's suggestion. I'd not thought to bring any with me, but she gushed about how pretty I looked in the dress, and offered me a selection of necklaces to go with it.

The weirdness hit me again when we got ready to leave for the steakhouse and I made straight for the passenger side of Lee's car.

'Oh,' he said. 'Um.'

'What's up?'

'Elle,' Noah called, 'why don't you come ride with us?'

I looked over at him, kind of baffled, because when had I ever *not* gone with Lee when the option was available? But then I noticed Rachel, clutching her purse and smiling awkwardly at me, and I got it. I brushed it off with an easy smile, saying, 'Sure!' – but it didn't stop me feeling like a stone had settled in the pit of my stomach.

When we got to the steakhouse and were seated, I ended up next to Rachel, with the boys opposite us. June and Matthew sat on the end by Lee and Rachel at least, so they took the brunt of the conversation. I was kind of glad. I still felt thrown by the whole situation with the cars earlier.

Even after we'd sat down, though, it was still different. Noah's leg was pressed against mine under the table, and every so often he'd reach across to do something like brush a strand of hair off my face or trace patterns on the back of my hand. He didn't usually do stuff like that around his family. Neither of us did. Even when the food came, and conversation lulled, there were moments when I'd look up because I felt him watching me – and he'd have this warm, intense look in his bright blue eyes. I had to gaze back down at my plate, poking my food around with a fork, trying not to blush.

Tonight was different, but I tried to tell myself that didn't have to be a bad thing. We were all having a good time. Everything was fine.

And everything *was* going fine, until we'd ordered dessert.

'Oh, hey!' Rachel said all of a sudden. 'I never said congrats on getting into Harvard, Flynn. That's so fantastic!'

Noah shifted ever so slightly. I only knew because I felt his knee bump against mine, but it was almost an imperceptible motion. 'Thanks. We're checking out the campus in a couple of days.'

'Didn't your cousin work at Harvard?' Lee said.

Rachel nodded. 'Yeah! He loved it there. He was just working in one of the dorms for a while, but he said everyone was really great, and the campus was really nice.'

Noah nodded. It was the indifferent, uninterested nod that was so typically Flynn – the badass persona Noah put out to everyone at school. I poked him with my foot below the table.

His dad seemed to notice that Noah had gone quiet and said, 'It's an amazing opportunity.'

'Exactly,' I added hastily, hoping my voice sounded reassuring. 'You'd have to be crazy to pass it up.'

Noah just looked at me.

Despite June talking to me about Noah going to Harvard at the end of the summer, I deliberately hadn't brought it up with him yet. We'd been having such a good time at the beach house, and it wasn't exactly like we'd had much time alone to talk about it.

I got the feeling from the look he gave me then that we really, really did need to talk about it.

I stole a glance at Lee, tearing my eyes from Noah's impenetrable gaze. My best friend shot me a sympathetic smile. I wished again that Noah was as easy to read as his brother.

'Lemon sorbet?' the waiter said, suddenly appearing with armfuls of carefully balanced plates.

'That's me.' Rachel put up her hand a little.

I looked at Noah again as dessert plates were handed out. I felt like I had to say *something* to break the tension between us.

In the end, I settled for, 'How's the food? It looks good. I should've ordered something.'

'Here.' A fork was suddenly pushed right in front of my face, a lump of cheesecake and gooey, delicious raspberry sauce on the end of it. 'See for yourself.'

I raised my eyebrows slightly at Noah, who was giving me a tiny smirk, one that tugged at the corners of his mouth, acting normal and ignoring the awkward atmosphere leftover from the college talk. I felt my cheeks warm up, but leaned in to take the bite.

I made an appreciative noise – the kind you make when food is melt-in-your-mouth, oh-my-gosh delicious, which made Noah grin at me. I swallowed, and bit back a laugh. My eyes crinkled with a suppressed smile.

Then Lee said, 'Ew, cooties,' and I burst out laughing, the others chuckling along with me. Forgetting the twist in my gut at the prospect of Noah and I breaking up in just a matter of weeks when he left, and the awkwardness that had been thick in the air before, I just enjoyed myself. Noah held my gaze with that intense look, a sparkle of amusement in his eyes and a mischievous quality to his smile. Even if I did have only a few more weeks with him, I knew I was lucky to have that much – even for just a little while.

I tidied up a few of my things, like dirty laundry and tossed-aside sandals, as Rachel was unpacking the rest of her stuff on the other side of the bedroom. She was telling me how excited she was about the next few days, and about spending some quality time with Lee and his family.

'I wouldn't bank on quality time with Lee,' I warned her with a laugh. 'That's pretty hard to come by here, with everyone around.'

'Guessing you're speaking from experience, there.'

'Yup. I don't think Noah and I have had more than, like, five minutes alone yet.'

A knock on the bathroom door cut our conversation short.

'You ladies decent?' Lee's voice was hushed, but muffled by the door; it was kind of hard to hear him. I rolled to the other side of my bed and leaned over to open the door.

'Now you're all polite because your girlfriend's here.'

Lee just grinned. 'But you know you don't really count as a girl, Shelly.'

I raised an eyebrow. 'What's up? Did you leave something in here, or are you just missing our room so much already?'

'Our room?' Rachel echoed. We both looked over to see her blinking at us, confusion all over her face. 'Did you guys ... I thought you and Noah shared this room?'

59

Lee laughed, reaching over to ruffle my hair. 'As if. Nah, me and Elle have always shared. Noah got his own room, since he's the oldest.'

'Oh. Oh, right. Sure.'

Rachel's usually bright smile seemed stiff, and she quickly turned back to plugging in her phone charger. I shot Lee a look. Didn't he ever mention, when he told her about the beach house, that we shared a room?

Not that it had ever mattered to us, but . . . Well, I could see how someone like *his girlfriend* might find it weird.

'I'm so glad to have a different room-mate for once,' I told Rachel, trying to lighten the mood. 'Someone who's, like, actually tidy. And doesn't snore.'

'Speak for yourself,' Lee told me. 'Anyway. I didn't come here to be insulted.' He lowered his voice to a whisper. 'I came because we're switching rooms.'

'Huh?' Rachel and I shared a look of confusion.

Lee rolled his eyes at me. 'Just get in there –' he jerked a thumb over his shoulder – 'for, like, an hour or something. I want to spend some alone time with my girlfriend, if you don't mind.'

I grinned, biting back a laugh. 'A connecting bathroom between you guys and us girls isn't exactly the best way for your parents to keep us separated, I guess.'

'What they don't know won't hurt them. We'll switch back in a bit. Now shoo.' Well, I didn't need to be told twice. Lee called quietly after me just before I disappeared into the bathroom, 'No hanky-panky, Shelly! These walls are thin.'

I snorted, and Rachel questioned, 'Hanky-panky, Lee? Seriously?'

I paused before I went into Noah's room, remembering I was in my pajamas. I didn't care so much that I had no make-up on; the past few days I hadn't bothered wearing any, since we'd been down at the beach. But the threadbare gray shorts and the shapeless navy tank top that fit me like a sack wasn't exactly the kind of thing I wanted my boyfriend to see me in.

I looked at myself in the mirror for a moment, then muttered, 'Whatever.' Noah had seen me in a worse state than this: he'd held my hair back for me when I got too drunk at a party and puked my guts into a toilet bowl. Compared to that, old pajamas were glamorous. When I yanked open the door to Noah's bedroom, though, I saw I didn't even need to worry if he thought I looked terrible in my pajamas. The room was almost pitch-black, so I could barely even make out the bed. I threw a hand to the wall, finding it after a few moments, and started walking forward tentatively, my other arm feeling around in front of me.

'Noah?' I whispered. I was afraid to talk too loudly in case we were all caught out.

'Polo,' he whispered back, chuckling under his breath. 'And you're supposed to say, "Marco", you know.'

I scowled slightly. 'Couldn't you have put the light on? I can't s–'

My foot caught the airbed that Lee was sleeping on. I crashed down, arms flailing. My elbow whacked the end of Noah's bed and I grunted as the air was knocked out of me. There was a long pause, like we were both waiting for someone to burst in.

'Ouch,' I mumbled, face in the airbed.

'Are you okay?' Noah whispered. I heard him climb off the bed.

'Fine. Just hit my funny bone. Ow. Lucky the airbed broke my fall.'

'Good.' And then, half laughing, he said, 'Klutz.'

'Jerk,' was my only comeback. He chuckled again and I felt a hand on my waist, an arm pressed against my back. His hand found mine, and I managed to get to my feet without falling over again.

'Sneaking around, Elle?' Noah said, mock-scolding me. His warm, spearmint breath tickled my face. I giggled quietly, and went to kiss him, but missed and ended up kissing his chin instead. He laughed, but then he kissed the side of my nose.

I bit my lip to muffle a snort, and Noah stepped back, pulling me along with him, until we were both sitting on the bed.

'How do you always manage to fall over, Elle?' he said, playing with the ends of my hair. My eyes now adjusted to the darkness, I could just about see Noah's face, and it looked like he was smiling. Not smirking, but giving me that smile that showed the dimple in his cheek.

I shrugged in answer. 'Guess I can't help falling for you.'

He chuckled, and his forehead rested against mine. 'You're such a romantic.'

'Is that bad?'

'Hmm, maybe. But not when it's you. When it's you, it's just cute.'

Suddenly his lips were pressed against mine, finding their target this time, and I curled my arms round his shoulders, trying to draw him closer. Noah's arms went round me, too, pulling me into him, until we were lying on our sides facing each other, our legs tangled up of their own accord.

'Your feet are freezing,' he commented.

'Maybe your feet are abnormally warm.'

'No, it's just you.'

I laughed again, trying not to be too loud. Then, in that ominous tone that told me he actually wanted to talk about something serious, he said, 'Elle.'

I had a feeling I knew what this was going to be about. I half hoped I was right, because we really did need to talk about it, to try and sort something out, but the rest of me wanted it to be something else, because there were so many things he might say that would break my heart.

'What?' I whispered back eventually.

'What ... what *are* we gonna do? When I go to college?'

He was waiting for me to answer him now. Even though it was dark enough that he probably couldn't really see my expression, I composed my face. I shrugged in his embrace. 'I don't know. I don't want you to –' I bit my tongue momentarily. 'I'm going to miss you.'

'I'm going to miss you too. But we should talk about what we're going to do when summer's over.'

Now was my chance – to say that we could at least *try* long distance, that we shouldn't call it off after summer just in case things didn't work out, kind of like his mom had said to me. But I was so afraid that he might not want to, that it might spoil the rest of the time we did have.

But before I'd made up my mind about what I should say, my mouth was already blurting out, 'We could try long distance. We could at least give it a shot.'

I stopped talking before I said something really stupid, like, *Unless you'd rather break up.* Luckily for me, Noah didn't seem to notice that my mind was freaking out more than a little bit.

'That's really what you want?' he asked.

'Yeah. I mean, is . . . isn't it what you want too?'

Great work, Elle, now he's going to say no, it's not what he wants, and the rest of the summer will be ruined. Good job.

'Of course it is! But – I mean, I feel like I'm being selfish, if that's not what you want. You'll be waiting around for me to come back for Thanksgiving and Christmas break. It's not fair on you that I'm all the way across the country in Massachusetts. That feels like a huge commitment, and I don't want to ask you to do that if you're . . . not . . . Like, if you don't . . .'

My heart skipped a beat.

He was more worried about me waiting for him to come back home than the fact he might meet someone who was prettier, smarter, all around better than me? He was worried that *I* was the one who wouldn't want to give a long-distance relationship a fair shot?

'What I don't want,' I said, propping myself up on my elbows and giving him a stern look he probably couldn't see, 'is to just break up, and make things easy.

Hell, Noah. When have we ever made things easy for ourselves?'

I could just about make out his smile. 'So . . .'

'You know, *I* was the one thinking *you* wouldn't want to do long distance,' I groaned, pressing my head into the crook of his neck. 'I think we should get better at talking to each other.'

'Talking is going to be pretty important when I'm on the other side of the country,' Noah agreed. His voice had taken on a low, husky quality, and he pulled me in closer, his lips finding my neck. 'But I can think of something pretty important for right now.'

'That so?' I teased.

Noah flipped us round so he was leaning over me, and I guessed it didn't matter how old my pajamas were when Noah was busy running a hand under my tank top, the two of us moving slowly, quietly, whispering in the dark, glad to finally have some time alone.

Chapter 7

The next day we ventured out to a more public part of the beach, and the boys joined in a game of volleyball that Rachel and I decided to sit out. Volleyball had never been my sport, but it really wasn't so bad when you were sitting on the side, watching. Especially when Noah looked even sexier than usual, what with the thin film of sweat on his broad shoulders, his dark hair flopping in his eyes, his abs . . .

He happened to glance over when I was staring at him through my gas-station sunglasses (which weren't dark enough to hide the fact that I was checking him out). He winked.

'Oh my gosh, did you see that?' some girl squealed all of a sudden from behind me. 'He totally just winked at me, right? I mean, that was so obvious, right? He *totally* winked at me.'

I looked at Rachel, who glanced back at the girl and raised her eyebrows at me.

'You should so get his number after,' another girl said. Rachel's eyebrows went up even higher. I could see her holding back a laugh. 'You have to. He was totally coming on to you.'

I turned round, and the two girls looked at me. They seemed at least two years older than me, probably in college. 'What?' one of them snapped.

'He wasn't winking at you. Just, you know, FYI.'

The girl snorted. 'Sure. What, you think he was winking at *you*?' She looked me up and down with the corner of her lip curled up.

'Um, yeah,' I replied.

'Oh, sure,' her friend scoffed. 'He was looking at *you*.'

'Well,' Rachel said, 'considering she's dating him, I'd say he *definitely* wasn't winking at you.'

I could hear the girls muttering behind us before getting up and stalking off. I grinned at Rachel, nudging her.

'Who knew Miss Sunshine could be such a badass? Remind me to never get on the wrong side of you!'

That night, Lee took Rachel out to see a movie and go for dinner afterward. There was an art gallery opening in the next town over, so Matthew and June went there. Which just left me and Noah alone in the beach house.

I was swimming lengths in the pool when he came out and tapped me on the shoulder.

'Did you forget about the special surprise I had planned for you?'

Crap. I totally had.

'Uh . . .'

'I'm cooking dinner. Which, hopefully, I won't burn.'

'You're cooking dinner?'

'Sure I am. Everyone else is out, which means . . . we've got date night.'

The words *date night* were all I needed to get me out of the pool and into the shower.

I had no idea what to wear; my only pretty dress, the yellow one, was in the laundry. I had shorts and T-shirts, sure, but nothing I really wanted for a *date*, if we were going to call it that.

I had no choice but to call Rachel.

'You're so lucky,' she answered. 'I just went to the bathroom; I was about to go back into the movie. What's wrong?'

'Noah's making dinner and I have nothing to wear.'

I was really only after her advice about what outfit to put together and how to dress it up appropriately, since she knew practically the entire wardrobe I'd brought to the beach house.

What I didn't expect her to say was, 'The white halter dress in my side of the closet. Wear those cute black sandals you brought too. Now I have to go – the guy at the popcorn stall is frowning at me. Bye!'

'I owe you,' I said, even though she'd hung up already. Hurrying, I found the dress she was talking about. I didn't have enough time to do much with my hair, so I threw it up into a ponytail. But when I looked in the mirror, I smiled. I actually looked pretty good, especially considering I'd only had thirty minutes to get ready.

I paused outside the kitchen, though, taking a deep breath and smiling to myself. When I breathed in, I could smell Noah's cooking. Whatever it was, it smelled great – if maybe a little burnt.

The kitchen light was off, but the soft light outside threw Noah's silhouette against the glass doors. Still smiling, I walked out, but hovered in the doorway.

'It's not that burnt,' he said, looking back at me. 'I swear.'

I laughed. 'I never said a word!'

He'd changed since I'd seen him when I'd walked past him earlier on my way to shower. He wore a pair of black jeans and a gray shirt that strained over his biceps. Even his messy dark hair was a little tidier than usual – like he'd run a comb through it. I found myself thinking he looked cuter and more carefree with it all messy, almost in his eyes. And, of course, he looked as hot as ever.

'You were thinking it,' he argued. 'I know it smells burnt. At least you can't really see it, though, because of the sauce . . .'

I laughed again. 'Who knew you were such a chef?'

He winked, a smirk stretching over his face. 'I'm a man of many talents, Elle, what can I say?'

'Don't get too arrogant,' I warned him.

'Yeah, you're right. Could give us food poisoning.'

'Exactly my thoughts,' I teased, and went round him to sit down. The food looked good – no, it looked delicious, and it actually smelled fantastic too. It was some kind of chicken casserole dish with vegetables and a thick reddish sauce.

The evening passed in a hazy blur of good food and laughter, my stomach fizzing every time Noah reached his hand out to mine.

After we finished dinner, we walked down the familiar path to the beach that we both knew by heart (which was just as well, given how dark it was already), our arms brushing against each other. At some point, our fingers interlocked too. Hand in hand like that, we walked down on to the beach.

The clouds had been gathering all afternoon and now blotted out the sky to a starless, inky black. The water was just as dark, the white foam of the waves breaking on the shore. Neither of us spoke as we strolled on the wet sand, the sea washing up and over our feet. I was carrying my sandals in my free hand, dangling them from my fingertips. Noah carried his flip-flops and had rolled his jeans up too.

And it was nice. Just being quiet, I mean. The only sound was the crashing water off to the side. You couldn't even hear any trace of distant traffic. There was the occasional bark of a dog, though – we weren't the only people taking a nighttime wander on the beach.

I loved it.

There was a grumble overhead.

I glanced up, craning my neck.

'It's probably not going to come to anything,' Noah said, meaning the thunder.

We walked along a little further before I said, 'Thank you. For doing all this, I mean.'

'All we're doing is walking on the beach.'

'No, I mean, cooking and stuff.'

He shrugged. 'It was just a casserole. Mom's recipe.'

'I mean it. This was a great date night. Thank you.'

I pulled Noah to a stop so I could lean up to kiss him.

Something cold and wet landed on my nose before I had a chance. Then another cold, wet thing landed on my temple, trickling down beside my eye.

Tilting my head back, I looked up almost at the same time as Noah.

Then, those threatening, rolling clouds just ripped open, and torrential rain started beating down on us all of a sudden. I let out a shriek of surprise. Noah was already running for shelter, dragging me behind him and going so fast I kept stumbling over my own feet. The sand we kicked up stuck on my legs, and my ponytail was coming loose too.

The rain hammered down, soaking me through to the bone. My hair stuck round my neck, or was plastered to my face where it had come loose from my ponytail. I could feel my mascara running, sticking my eyelashes together.

We made it back up to the beach house, Noah ushering me in first and hauling the door closed behind us.

We were both breathing hard and dripping water on to the floor. Thunder rumbled again outside.

'You know you said this was a great date night?'

I looked over at Noah and we both burst out laughing.

Lovesick as it sounds, I felt almost hypnotized by him in that moment. Everything about him was perfect in my eyes – from the look he was giving me, to the way he was so much taller than me, even to his crooked nose.

'I love you.'

He looked even more handsome with that smile in his eyes lighting up his face. He didn't answer me, instead stepping closer, his lips crashing down on mine and his hands cupping my face. I didn't need him to say anything, I realized. Noah might not be as easy to read as Lee, but right now, I knew everything I needed to.

Chapter 8

'Rachel's gone, then, huh?'

'Yep,' Lee answered. 'Back to just the three of us now. At least for a couple more days.'

The last few days with Rachel had been nice, but it had still felt weird. I hadn't been able to shake the feeling things weren't quite right. And I knew it wasn't fair to not want her around when I was a huge part of why things were different. I knew I'd spent less time with Lee and more with Noah – and that, really, it was a good thing Rachel had been here, to help distract from that fact.

But still, I wasn't too sorry she'd left, giving me a little while longer at the beach house with the Flynn boys.

'Just like old times.' I grinned.

'I guess I won't be coming back here for the next few years,' Noah said suddenly. 'This might be my last summer here.'

I didn't think I'd ever heard Noah sound so sad. He tried to hide it, though, and coughed abruptly – like that'd cover up the emotion his voice betrayed. 'And next year will probably be your last year, too, and Lee's.'

'Why?' Lee demanded. 'We're coming back every year. Just like we always do.'

Noah scoffed. 'Don't count on it. You guys can try, but it's probably not gonna happen that way. Pessimist, I know, I know,' he said, cutting across me as I started to tell him he was being stupid and cynical. 'But what about summer internships? Jobs? You've got it pretty cushy now, but that's gonna change at some point. Not everything has a happily ever after.'

What about us? What about our happily ever after?

I bit my lip and decided not to say anything. I knew that wasn't what he'd meant by it. We were going to give it our best shot. I couldn't ask for more than that.

'Look at him.' Lee nudged my arm and pointed across to Noah. 'Thinking he's all wise now he's old enough to go to college; thinking he's got it all figured out. Noah, if you think that we're not dragging your ass back to this place every summer, you are sadly mistaken. Summer is *all* about coming here.'

'You know, Lee, one day, you're gonna grow up too.'

'Never. Remember that time in fifth grade when I played Peter Pan in the school play? There's a reason they picked me.'

Noah sighed, but I cut him a look that said, *Don't push it.* The last thing I wanted right then was for the two of them to start arguing – because much as that might feel like old times, I would really rather not be in the middle of it. Hoping to distract them both, and not wanting Lee to sulk about the prospect of a summer without the beach house, I grabbed the football we'd brought with us.

'Come on, then, Lee. You said you've been practicing.' I threw the ball at him. 'Show us what you've got.'

'Jeez, Lee, could you make any more mess? I think I liked it better when Rachel was my room-mate.' I wrinkled my nose at some underwear near my bed, kicking it over to Lee's side of the room. He'd moved back in now Rachel had gone.

'You don't think it's weird we still share a room, right?' I asked him, remembering Rachel's reaction that first night she was here. 'You don't think we're too old for that?'

'Shelly, I carry tampons in my school backpack for you. We passed weird, like, five years ago.' He scooped

77

up some of his laundry and paused to look at me. 'You don't think it's weird, do you?'

'Of course I don't. It was just – I don't know. Rachel seemed to think it was.'

'Nah. She knows we're not like that.'

I pulled a face while I still had my back to him, not convinced. I wasn't sure how I'd feel about it if I were in Rachel's shoes, but – well, it was *Lee*. This was just how we were.

'Hey, you guys set for tomorrow?' Noah asked, leaning through the bedroom doorway.

It would be our last day together – Noah was leaving the next day. So, despite not being a morning person, I'd set alarms to make sure I was up early. I was going to make the most of these final few hours, whatever it took.

'We will be,' Lee said. 'Though Elle's going to need a while to get her face on and fix that bedhead.'

I patted my hair. I knew it would need taming down tomorrow, but scrabbled about on the dresser for a hair tie to pull it back into a ponytail now.

'Don't listen to him, Elle. You look great.'

I blew Noah a kiss. 'You don't look so bad yourself.'

Lee made an exaggerated gagging sound. 'If you two are done flirting, can we say goodnight?'

I giggled, and threw the T-shirt and sock of his I was still holding at his head. The sock caught on his ear until he shook it off, like a dog. Noah chuckled too, and that wistful part of me, the part that was forever a hopeless romantic, wished I could take a snapshot of the moment – all three of us laughing and smiling at the beach house together like always, and seemingly without a care in the world.

It was a perfect moment in time – but that's all it was. A moment.

Chapter 9

Our last day together went by way too quickly. We'd tried to cram everything in: games of Frisbee, tossing a football around, swimming in the ocean, playing volleyball (I'd joined in this time, even if I was awful at it). Noah and I had left Lee playing another round of volleyball to get some time to ourselves at the beach bar – thankfully without any problems like the last time.

I wished it could have lasted forever. I wished Noah didn't have to leave.

I was dreading saying goodbye to him. I knew it wasn't for long, and he'd be back soon, but it just made me think about how much harder it would be to say goodbye when he left for good. I was trying really hard not to think about it; it was dragging down my happy mood.

'Mm,' Lee said, pulling me out of my thoughts, 'I just remembered!'

Except he was talking with his mouth full, so it sounded more like, *Mmmph, ah jush muh-mem-phud*. I understood what he was saying, though; after seventeen years of being around Lee, I'd got used to listening to him tell me things with his mouth full of food.

'What?' I said – *after* I'd swallowed my food.

'Well,' he said, gulping down his burrito loudly, then belching even louder. 'You know this morning when we were playing volleyball? After you guys left, I was talking to a couple of guys. There's a party down on the beach tomorrow night. There's gonna be a whole bunch of people there. But no bonfire, they said.'

'They haven't had a bonfire for years,' Noah said, but he sounded uninterested – or distracted. 'The police caught them a few years back. Something about a safety hazard.'

'A safety hazard right by the sea?' I said.

He shot me a flat look, but then turned back to Lee. 'So? What's your point?'

Lee took another impossibly huge bite of his burrito. This time, he swallowed most of it before he answered. 'Well . . . my point is, there's a party tomorrow. So, me and Shelly can go.'

'Really?' My pulse picked up and I felt my eyebrows shooting toward my hairline. We hadn't been to a beach party before. They'd been something that Noah would disappear to one or two nights, but Lee and I had always been too young. June and Matthew (and my dad, via phone call) hadn't let us go when Noah was going. And Noah hadn't wanted us there.

There was that one year, when we were fourteen: we'd snuck down to the party even after my dad and Lee's parents had told us we were 'not allowed to go'. Mostly, though, we snuck down to spy on Noah. It hadn't been very successful, though. He'd caught us trailing after him and threatened to phone his mom and tell on us.

Childish, but it worked.

We probably would've been allowed to go last year, maybe even the year before, but we'd never asked. The parties were Noah's thing. Lee and I stayed at the house playing video games and joking about, like we always did.

Now, though, adrenaline coursed through me.

'Really?' I squealed. 'We get to go to a beach party this year? We're going to a party –'

'Um,' Noah interrupted. 'I don't think so.'

'What?' Lee and I both turned on him, wide-eyed with pure confusion.

'Do you even know what goes on at those things?' he said. I pursed my lips, glaring at him. If he was going to turn right back into an overprotective jerk . . .

'We're going,' I told him.

'Elle.' He sighed, with a look on his face that I completely ignored.

'No, she's right,' Lee interrupted. 'I'm going. And Shelly can't not go if I go. Therefore, we are both going.' I was so tempted to make a comment like, *Therefore? Wow, that's a pretty big word for you, Lee*, but I was too interested in what he had to say. 'Besides, you can't keep track of where she's going and what she's doing every single day.'

'Well, the beauty of Instagram means I kind of can,' Noah joked. 'But I'm serious. You guys have never been to one of these parties. They can get really crazy. There's alcohol, douchey guys . . . Things can get pretty wild. I swear I saw drugs getting passed around last year. And I'm not talking about weed.'

'Oh, come on.' Lee snorted. 'As if we're going to get involved in anything like that.'

'Some of those parties get out of control real quick, Lee. I can handle myself. I'm not so sure about you guys.'

'We're not idiots, Noah.'

'You don't even know the guys who invited you.'

'Sure I do. I added one of them on Facebook.'

'Elle,' Noah said, turning to me now. 'Are you serious about this? You really wanna go that bad? I'm telling you guys, it's not your scene –'

'You're not the boss of her,' Lee interrupted.

'Yeah, well, neither are you.'

'I'm her best friend,' Lee snapped. 'I'll take care of her just fine.'

'And I'm her boyfriend,' Noah retorted. 'I'm trying to look out for her.'

I stood up and walked off.

That got their attention. Lee called, 'Shelly!' and Noah said, 'Elle?'

I carried on stalking away from our little evening picnic on the beach. I didn't walk very far, though, getting only a few feet away before I spun back round.

'Okay,' I said. 'Look, Lee and I are going to that party tomorrow, and neither of us are going to do anything stupid. We'll be careful. And I appreciate you, both of you, looking out for me, but – newsflash – I don't need either of you cataloging my every move and babysitting me. Got that?'

It was hard to tell who looked more stunned by my outburst – Lee or Noah. I was pretty stunned myself, since I hadn't expected to rant at them like that when I'd opened my mouth.

Lee recovered first, though. 'Sorry.'

'Fine,' Noah said. 'But just promise me you guys will get out of there if things start heading south. Both of you.'

It was sweet, I thought, that he wasn't only worried about me. I'd been ready to argue with him, thinking he was being kind of a jerk telling us not to go, but he was just looking out for us. Both of us.

'We swear,' I told him. 'Right, Lee?'

Lee huffed, but said, 'Yeah, we swear. We'll be careful.'

I sat back down, reaching for some chips. I caught Lee's eye and grinned at him. 'Hey, Lee . . . beach party.'

He beamed back at me. *'Beach party.'*

Chapter 10

'I'll be home when you guys get back,' Noah said, his arms tightening round me. 'Time's going to fly by.'

It sounded kind of like he was trying to convince himself of that as well as me, so I just squeezed him tighter and rested my head against his shoulder. I heard the *clunk-click* sound of the trunk closing as Matthew finished loading his and Noah's luggage into the car.

Lee and June were still standing on the doorstep, waiting for them to leave. They'd been waiting there at least ten minutes to wave Matthew and Noah off, since they'd already said their goodbyes. And besides, it wasn't like they'd be gone for long.

'I bet I'll hate it there,' Noah said, still trying to cheer me up. 'I'll be desperate to come back here.'

'I doubt it,' I mumbled into his shirt.

'Oh, come on. A bunch of preppy guys in sweater-vests and tweed? Not my kind of crowd.'

I laughed at his attempt at humor, but it felt fake and I had a feeling it sounded fake. So I tried to smile instead, but it felt a bit more like a grimace.

'Shut up,' I told him instead. 'You'll love it there.'

'Sure. I'll just love being surrounded by a bunch of do-gooders.'

I leaned away just far enough to swat at his chest, this time the smile on my face genuine, if only a small one. 'Yeah, yeah. Because you're so ruthless and villainous, now, aren't you?'

'Love does wonders to hurt a guy's rep, huh?' He gave me a kiss for what must have been the billionth time that morning.

If things hadn't been so different this year, I wouldn't have cared as much that he was going away for a few days. I could handle spending a little while without my boyfriend; that wasn't the problem.

The thing was, it was all so wrong. The fact that Noah and his dad were leaving us early was just *not right*.

Summers at the beach house were supposed to be all of us together just having fun, spending a while without worrying about our lives back home. Summers at the beach house weren't supposed to be cut short by trips to college campuses. It just felt too grown-up.

I remembered our conversation from the other day – Noah wondering if this would be his last summer here, that it might soon be our last summer here too.

Lee might have convinced himself that it would never happen, but I wasn't so sure.

Things were already changing so much. What if they only got worse?

'Time to go, Noah.'

And speaking of things getting worse . . .

My gut twisted. There was a lump in the back of my throat. I had that prickly feeling behind my eyes, like you get when you're about to cry. My palms got all clammy. My breath shuddered when I exhaled.

If this was what I felt like just thinking of him leaving for college, how was I ever going to cope when the time came for him to go *for real*?

Almost as though he was able to read my thoughts, Noah smoothed my hair back off my face, and left his hand lingering, his thumb stroking my cheek lightly. His electric blue eyes bored into mine with a look so intense I could only stare back and wonder what *he* was thinking.

'Be careful at this party, okay?' he murmured.

I nodded. 'Don't worry about me.'

'I do. A lot. You're the kind of person who needs to be worried about. Especially being as clumsy as you are. And with Peter Pan over there being such a bad influence.'

I laughed, and when I met his eyes again, the corner of his mouth twitched up in a smile. 'I'll be careful, don't worry. We both will. I'll look after him.'

'Good.' He kissed my forehead again.

'Have fun in Massachusetts.'

'Mm,' he said doubtfully, but smiled. 'I'll try.'

Noah gave me one final kiss, but I think we were both hyper-aware of the fact that his parents and his brother were waiting for us to finish up saying goodbye, so it was only a brief one. But it was still enough of a kiss to send the fireworks thrill through me.

I spent another few melancholy moments standing with Noah, saying goodbye, before scuttling back up to the porch, where Lee and his mom were waiting.

I'd always thought it was kind of pathetic how couples took forever to say goodbye – and then started the whole thing over again. It seemed like some big, sappy, over-exaggerated thing that even the hopeless romantic in me didn't really appreciate too much. But now it was happening to me, I understood. You did it because you wanted to delay them leaving you as long as possible. You did it to try and stall the future. Buy a few more seconds with them.

As soon as I set foot on the porch, Lee grabbed my hand and squeezed it hard. I wasn't crying, but he seemed to know how heavy my heart felt without the need for tears pouring down my face. I glanced sideways at him, catching his eye and giving him a small, grateful smile. It was comforting to know that, whatever happened, I always had Lee.

'Call me when you get there!' June yelled after them as her husband reversed off the sand-covered driveway. He held up a hand – a gesture that said, *Yeah, sure thing!* but the look on his face was one that said, *I didn't hear you, but whatever!*

Once the sound of the car engine had died away round the bend of the street that led toward the highway, June let out a sigh and went back inside. Lee let go of my hand.

'Forget about you,' my best friend said in mock-horror, 'how am *I* going to cope when he goes off to college and leaves you behind?'

His expression, which was bug-eyed and aghast, made me laugh a little. 'I won't be all heartbroken and depressed, don't worry. Besides, we have a party to go to tonight!'

'Yeah!' His hand went up for a high five – then he dropped his arm just before I could slap my hand against his. 'Aw, man! Shelly, *please* tell me this doesn't mean I have to take you shopping!'

'Well . . .' I laughed before he could roll his eyes. 'Kidding.'

'Thank God! I get enough of it at home. This is the beach house. It's for skinny-dipping, not buying lots of clothes. Or, I guess, in your case it'd be chunky-dunking.'

'Hey!'

He laughed, grinning impishly. 'See, I've already brightened you up, my heartbroken little friend.'

'I'm not heartbroken.'

'Not yet, because you're in denial.'

'What?' I laughed. 'I'm not in denial, and I'm not heartbroken. I'll see him in a couple of days – there's nothing to be heartbroken over right now.'

He gave me a disbelieving look.

Then, 'Just so you know, Elle, if he ever does break your heart – I'm there.'

I squeezed his arm. 'You're the best best friend a girl could ask for.'

Chapter 11

I figured a beach party couldn't be too fancy, so it didn't take me long to get ready. A pair of shorts and a white cami, and I was good to go.

'It's gonna be cold,' Lee reminded me.

'Right,' I said, snapping my fingers. I picked up the gray zip-up hoodie lying across my pillow, and then slipped my feet into my sandals. 'Okay! Now I'm ready!'

Lee swung himself off from where he was lying across his bed with his hair grazing the floor. He was wearing dark khakis and a plain white T-shirt, and had a hoodie exactly like mine (my gray hoodie used to belong to Lee, actually. But I kept stealing it because it was so comfy, and in the end he bought a new one).

'Come on, then,' he said, linking his arm through mine.

'You kids off, now, huh?' June asked as we wandered through the lounge to go out of the back door. The TV was on, but she was wrapped up in the mystery novel she'd been working her way through for the past few days.

'Yup,' we answered simultaneously.

'Okay, well, have fun. But *be careful*.' She'd already read us the riot act on not accepting drinks from anyone, not letting our own drinks out of our sight, not getting too drunk, how dangerous it could be, not to go too near the water, to stay together at all times ... It was like we'd never been to any party before. 'What time do you think you'll be back?'

'I don't know,' Lee said. 'Probably not much later than midnight, I guess. But don't wait up.'

She gave us a wry kind of smile. 'You think I'll be able to sleep easy if you're out at a party?'

'Noah's been going to them for years,' Lee pointed out. I could hear the slight irritation in his voice, like he was annoyed his mom wasn't letting him do things Noah had always done.

'And?' She laughed. 'I never got to sleep until he got home.'

There was a moment's pause, then Lee said, 'Oh.'

'Don't be too late,' June told us, the severe-mom look back on her face.

We both nodded. 'All right.'

'Have fun!' she trilled, turning back to her book and mug of coffee. (I guessed it wasn't decaf, if she was really going to stay up until we got home.)

'See you later,' we called back, and slid the doors closed behind us.

The night was warm, and the sky was clear. The flashing lights of an airplane went across the sky, and there were stars twinkling up there too, against the inky backdrop. It made me smile. I wanted to spin around in a circle, with my face tilted up to the sky.

I could feel Lee grinning at me.

'Go for it.'

So I did. Laughing, I spun around in circles with my arms flung out all the way down the beaten sandy path between the shrubbery until I lost my footing and fell over into a bush.

Lee was laughing too, and jogged over to give me a hand up.

It wasn't hard to find the party. It was a little past eight, but there were a lot of people around. There were coolers, and a couple of small campfires. People had dragged some logs round to make circles, and if they weren't sitting down, then they were milling about.

'This is the dangerous, drug-fueled rave your brother warned us to stay away from?' I couldn't help but ask incredulously, looking on. From here, it all seemed pretty tame.

As we got closer, I saw that the people there were mostly around college age; a little older than us. But there were a ton of kids our age too, and a few younger.

'Come on,' I said, grabbing Lee's hand and dragging him toward the nearest box of ice and beer cans. 'I'm thirsty.'

'What happened to, *No, I won't drink at all, don't worry*?'

'I never said that. I said I wouldn't get *drunk*. There's a difference.' I bent down and grabbed two cans of beer out of the slowly melting ice, handing one to Lee.

'Hey, Lee, you made it!' We turned around and saw a guy walking up to us.

'Hey,' Lee replied, doing that weird half-hug thing guys do. 'This is my friend I was telling you about, Elle. Elle, this is Kory.'

I sipped my beer. 'Hi.'

'You guys good for drinks? Come on,' Kory said. 'I'll introduce you to some people.'

And he did. Kory's group of friends all looked either our age, or maybe freshmen and sophomores at college. I was kind of able to put names to faces, but I'd forgotten half of them within the first few minutes.

At one point, while we were talking to some of them, Lee stood beside me and slung his arm round my shoulders. He drained the last of his can and said, 'I'm getting another drink – you want one?'

'No, I'm good.'

He ruffled my hair and walked off, one of the guys joining him. The other girl in our little group, Jess, watched them go for all of three seconds before saying, 'So, what, are you guys dating, or . . . ?'

'What?' I snorted. 'No way! Are you for real?'

She shrugged. 'You two just look pretty cozy.'

I laughed. 'You've got to be kidding. He's my *friend*. Not in a million years would we ever be – you know, *dating*.'

'Nothing wrong with being friends first,' one of the guys whose name I couldn't remember said. 'It's like the start of any great rom-com.'

I rolled my eyes. 'Not me and Lee. Trust me.'

I wasn't used to people asking about me and Lee. Everyone at school knew we'd always been practically joined at the hip, that we came as a package deal. I'd never really thought how it looked to an outsider.

I was still laughing about it by the time Lee came back.

Chapter 12

It was late, and a few people had started to leave the party. The alcohol supply had mostly run out, and the buzz it had given people seemed to be fading.

'Okay,' Kory announced, heaving himself up from where he lay on the ground. He shook the sand out of his hair with one hand. 'This is starting to get boring. Come on.'

So we did. We all got up and followed him a little further away from the clusters of partygoers to a small dying campfire a little further off, where we sat around on some logs.

After dumping a little more driftwood that was lying around near us on to the fire, a guy called Miles said, 'Truth or dare?'

'Sure,' everyone said, nodding. I wriggled into a more comfortable spot on the log, and hooked my arm through Lee's, feeling the chill of the night air now, glad he'd reminded me to bring a hoodie.

'I'll go first!' Jess chirped. 'Um . . . Maria! Truth or dare?'

'Truth.'

'Your most embarrassing moment. And don't spare us any details.'

Maria's olive cheeks turned pink. 'Right. Okay. Ugh, I hate you for this. Right. So, in my sophomore year of high school, some kid tripped me up in the canteen and I, um, I spilled my lunch all over the head cheerleader.'

'It doesn't stop there.' Jess giggled. 'Go on.'

Maria shot her a glare, but smiled a little. 'My pants ripped when I fell.'

There was a moment of silence. Then we all burst out laughing.

'Oh my gosh,' I gasped. 'Are you serious?'

'Honestly, girl, I wish I wasn't. My turn,' Maria said. 'But, Jess, I am going to get you back for that one later. Hmm, who should I . . . Miles.'

'Yep.'

'Truth or dare?'

'Dare.'

'I dare you . . . to . . . Oh God, I'm terrible at dares! Someone else think of one.'

'I've got one,' a boy called Hunter put in. 'See those guys over there?' He pointed and we all looked around. Miles nodded. 'Go pants one of them.'

Miles's eyebrows went up. 'Those guys are huge.'

Hunter shrugged. 'Probably drunk, though.'

Miles sighed. 'If I get a black eye, dude, you are so getting your ass kicked.'

We all watched as Miles walked over to the group of guys. He kept looking back over his shoulder like he was expecting one of us to tell him he didn't have to go through with the dare. But the guys didn't notice him as he got closer.

Then, in one hurried motion, he yanked the khakis of the closest guy down and spun round, sprinting for the safety of our little campfire so fast he fell face first into the sand and did a forward roll. My eyes widened in panic, wondering if he was all right.

He was back on his feet in a second, though, and his legs flailed around madly as he made his way toward us. The guy whose pants were now round his ankles was either too stunned or simply too drunk to pull them back up before trying to run after Miles. At that point, I had to laugh. Lee fell off the log because he was laughing so hard, and I wasn't the only one clutching my sides as Miles collapsed back in his spot.

'My . . . turn,' he panted. 'Nathan, truth or dare?'

And on it went. After we cracked open the supplies Jess had brought along to make s'mores, Lee was dared to fit as many marshmallows in his mouth as he could.

(For the record, it was fourteen.) I had a truth – what was my first kiss? It was fun, though, and when it came to truths, I didn't have a problem with sharing stuff with these random people, however embarrassing. I would never really see them again, so why should I care what they thought of me?

Everything was going great, until Hunter said, 'Elle. Truth or dare?'

And I replied, 'Dare. No! No, wait, truth!'

'Too late,' Kory said in an irritating sing-song voice. 'You already said dare.'

'I dare you,' Hunter said, 'to go skinny-dipping.'

I blinked. Then I blinked again. Eventually I said, 'Huh?'

'You know, skinny-dipping,' he repeated. 'In the sea.'

I looked round, over my shoulder, at the sea. It was as dark as the sky; the only way I could distinguish between them was by the white, foamy tips of waves.

'Um,' I said, fiddling with the zipper on my hoodie. 'Yeah, no thanks.' It was pitch-black out there – not to mention freezing in the water. And I was not about to *actually* skinny-dip. I'd almost tried to at one of Lee and Noah's parties once, after too many drinks. I'd never been so embarrassed.

Lee piped up, 'There's no way she's doing that. What if she drowned? Are you as big an idiot as you look?'

Hunter scowled at Lee. 'What the hell's it got to do with you, huh? It's no big deal. Everyone does it.'

Lee shook his head. 'Wow,' he scoffed. 'You're actually an even *bigger* idiot than I had you pinned for.'

Hunter shot to his feet.

Lee was standing in the next split second.

The two of them just stood there, glaring at each other.

'Hey – you don't have to be a substitute Noah,' I muttered, but loud enough that Lee heard me, since the rest of our little circle was so hushed. 'One is enough.'

I saw something flash across my best friend's face. It was somewhere between amusement and wanting to roll his eyes at me. But he fought hard to keep on glaring at Hunter.

'Fine,' Hunter snapped, sitting back down. 'You can do the forfeit.'

'I'll do the forfeit,' I said.

'You guys have to make out, that's the forfeit,' Jess said hastily, before Hunter had a chance to open his mouth.

'*What?*' I exclaimed, my head whipping round to look at Hunter. 'You're joking. Absolutely no way in hell that's happening.'

'Not Hunter,' Jess clarified, grinning. 'You and Lee.'

'*What?*' Lee and I both cried out that time. I added, 'Now I know you're joking.'

'Nuh-uh.' Nathan shook his head, his smile growing a little. 'Your forfeit is to kiss Lee.'

'Why am I involved in this?' Lee demanded.

'You were fine with getting involved a minute ago,' Hunter muttered at him.

'Yeah, but –' I started.

Lee said, 'I have a girlfriend, though. I can't –'

'And I have a boyfriend.'

'So what?' Kory shrugged. 'Neither of them are here, right? And it's just one harmless dare. Nobody even has to know.'

'Did he really just say that?' Lee asked nobody in particular.

'Did you have to?' I whined, turning to Jess. 'Really?'

She arched an eyebrow at me. 'Would you have preferred Hunter to give you a forfeit?'

'I guess not,' I mumbled back. 'But –'

'You two look so close. I mean, seriously. Tell me. Have you ever even tried it?'

'No, because –'

'Well, then, you'll never know. If it is true love, you can thank me later.' Then, loud enough that the others could hear her, she said, 'Come on, you two, don't chicken out on us now. Suspense is building. Tension is high. All that jazz.'

I turned to look at Lee.

'Um,' he said.

'Um,' I replied.

I searched his face, and I knew he was thinking the exact same thing as me: *This is not happening.*

I couldn't kiss him. It was way too –

'There.'

I blinked, and I missed it. I don't think he even really put his lips on my cheek long enough for it to constitute a kiss.

'No, that doesn't count!' Damien told us teasingly. 'That was barely the kind of kiss you give your grandma. Man up.'

They were all egging us on, drumming their knees and shouting.

Even if we were both totally and completely single, I knew there was no way I could ever kiss Lee.

What if it made things permanently weird between us? What if it wrecked everything?

Also – neither of us was single. I never backed down from dares usually, but this was different. I wasn't about to kiss *anybody* else, especially not for some stupid dare, to shut up people that I'd never see again.

And Lee had to be thinking the same, surely.

I heard Lee sigh, and because he was sitting so close to me I felt his breath wash over my face and neck; it sent a shiver down my spine.

'Well,' he mumbled, low enough for only me to hear. 'They can never tell us we didn't try it.'

And I just thought, *He's going to kiss me.*

Chapter 13

My first kiss had been with Noah, at the kissing booth. He'd tasted of spearmint and cotton candy, and I'd been totally lost because I'd never kissed a guy before. And, sure, I'd got in a lot of practice since then, but Noah was still the only guy I'd ever kissed.

Lee would taste like beer and marshmallows. I could smell it on his breath, he was that close. My eyes were shut tight and I could feel my mouth twisted into a thin line too.

I'd been so sure he was going to kiss me . . . but he didn't. I peeled my eyes back open and he was still right in front of me, his face scrunched up just like mine. 'Nope. Too weird.'

Everyone around us shouted again. *Go on, just one kiss, do it!*

'Your face looks strange this close.'

'So does yours. You have a booger, by the way,' I told him.

'You have a pimple under your nose.'

Far from kissing me, he reached up as if to squeeze the pimple for me – I knew he was joking around, but I still shrieked and twisted away – accidentally headbutting him in the process.

'Ow!' he exclaimed, pulling away. 'Shelly!'

'That was so your fault!'

He tackled me, pinning me down in the sand. He sat on my legs and pinned my arms over my head.

'Get off, you're getting sand in my hair!' I thrashed around, trying to break free. 'You're too heavy!'

'Payback!'

'Lee!'

'Elle!' he mimicked in a falsetto voice that sounded nothing like me. I frowned, but stopped wriggling, since I was getting nowhere, and Lee bent down so his mouth was right beside my ear.

'Was it just me or would that have been totally weird?'

I let out a breath of laughter. 'Definitely not just you,' I whispered back, smiling.

He chuckled a little, sounding as relieved as me.

And never mind it being totally bizarre, it would have been totally screwed up of me to kiss my boyfriend's brother.

'Lee.'

'What?'

'You're kind of crushing me.'

'So long as you're not suddenly crushing *on* me, Elle, it's all good.' He winked, jumping up and giving me a hand. 'You wanna head off?'

I was glad he'd suggested it, and nodded. The party had been good, but the fun was definitely over now. I was done with truth or dare.

'We're gonna shoot off,' Lee announced. 'I mean, you know, after that hot and heavy make-out session, we just can't keep our hands off each other. Gotta go find a room, you know?'

I snorted, and a few people got up to hug us goodbye, telling us to come again next time. Lee and I waved to the others and made our way back down the beach. I looped my arm through his, resting my head on his shoulder.

Thinking Lee had been about to kiss me had been weird beyond belief, but, in a way, I was glad we'd been given the stupid dare. It was as though now I knew for certain that there could never ever be anything romantic between us. And I liked that, I really, honestly did. I wanted things to always be the same with us, however many ups and downs and arguments. We'd made it the hardest seventeen years of our lives, and anyone who said we'd stop being friends later in life, or would always wonder *what if*, didn't know anything about us.

The next evening was our last, so our final dinner was made up of leftovers – meaning mostly salad and ice cream. The three of us put the house back in order, cleaning up before going to pack our things.

I'd always had trouble packing for the beach house.

Always.

And, I had to admit, I hated the repacking the night before we left the beach house just as much. It was always kind of a downer every year, but this year felt even worse than ever. Aside from the usual melancholy sight of our bedroom without all the clutter and clothes, and the simple fact that it was our last night here this year, it just felt so lonely, especially with Noah and his dad already gone.

Lee and I had said we'd come here every summer of our lives. But now it hit me – and it hit me hard – that the others might not be coming back with us.

And I really, really didn't like that.

It was a stupid thing to cry over, I guess. It was just a house. But was it really so terrible of me to want this one thing to stay the same forever?

And this place was so much more than a house. It was where we'd spent every summer since we were kids. It was the one place that, no matter how far apart Lee and Noah had drifted, they would (for the most part) get along. It was the one place where we could act like five-year-olds and not give a damn.

'I hate this,' Lee said quietly. He had his back to me, and was cramming shoes into nonexistent spaces in his suitcase. But he said it like he knew I was almost about to cry. 'The leaving, I mean. I hate the leaving.'

'Yeah.'

'We'll be back in a year. It's stupid to miss it.'

'I know, but it won't be the same, will it? Especially if Noah doesn't come. And we'll be, like, off to colleges . . .'

'Hey, what happened to our pact? We pinky promised when we were ten years old to come here every year, and now you want to break that promise? Shelly, you of all people should know how tightly the pinky promise binds you.'

I giggled, but it stuck in my throat. 'You know what I mean.'

'Kinda.' Then he sighed. 'It sucks, huh?'

'Definitely.'

After a few minutes passed, Lee's arms curled round me and he hugged me from behind. His chin was on my shoulder. After a couple of seconds, I turned and wrapped my arms round him, burying my face in his shoulder. We stood there like that, totally silent and holding each other.

I think Lee was just as upset as me, really, but he wasn't going to show it. I knew him too well, though. I didn't need him to tell me that Noah's comment about growing up and maybe not coming back had stuck with him too.

Right then, we both needed the hug.

And afterward, it was like the world felt a little brighter and a little warmer. I didn't feel quite so sad about the fact that this year could be the last we were all here for summer at the beach house together.

Because yeah, things changed.

And yeah, we still had a lot of growing up to do.

But, right then, everything I was worried about – from what would happen with me and Noah, to the stuff deeper down, like college, like the future – just didn't really matter any more.

I'd have to deal with those things at some point, but not right now. Not while we still had the beach house.

'Where are we going?' Lee asked as I started tugging him wordlessly out of the bedroom.

I didn't answer him.

'Shelly,' Lee asked again.

'Just wait,' I said, a grin spreading so wide over my face, I probably looked like I was doing an impression of the Cheshire Cat. I kicked off my flip-flops and Lee followed my lead. He was in old sweatpants and a T-shirt, and I was in some thin shorts and a tank top.

'Ready?' I asked.

He'd caught on by now, and all of a sudden the two of us were clattering through the house hand in hand, bumping into each other and into walls until we were outside, heading straight for the pool. Lee was beaming almost as widely as I was, and his eyes were lit up like Christmas trees. We drew to a stop at the edge of the pool, Lee holding me back as I teetered at the edge.

'Ready.' He winked and grabbed my hand. I linked my fingers tightly through his.

'Three . . . two . . .'

Then, at the same time, laughing and smiling because right then, we really didn't have a care in the world, we both yelled at the top of our lungs, *'Cannonball!'* and with a huge splash, jumped in at the deep end.

NEED TO KNOW WHAT HAPPENS NEXT?

Turn over to read the opening
of *The Kissing Booth 2:
Going the Distance*

Chapter 1

'Senior year, baby!'

Once the car door slammed shut behind me, I tilted back my head and let my eyes slide closed, drawing in a deep breath. The sun tickled my cheeks, and a smile played on my lips. The school smelled of freshly cut grass, and the air was filled with the bubbly chatter of teenagers running around the parking lot, meeting up with their classmates again after summer. Everybody always complained about how much they hated the first day of school – I was sure that everyone secretly loved it, though.

There was just something about the new school year that meant new beginnings. Which was kind of ridiculous, because it was *high school*, but it didn't stop it feeling true.

I turned to Lee, eyes open again now, and he shot me a grin.

It may have been a Monday morning, but I felt

weightless. My smile mirrored his. 'Senior year, here we come,' I replied softly.

If there was anything worth being excited about, I was sure that the start of senior year was it.

I'd heard people say that your college years were supposed to be the best years of your life – but college sounded like it was going to be so much more hard work than high school, even if it did mean more freedom. Lee and I were convinced that senior year was the last year to *really* enjoy ourselves, before adulthood hit.

I moved round the car to lean against the hood, next to Lee. He'd always made a fuss about his precious car, the '65 Mustang he cherished so dearly; hell, it practically sparkled.

'I can't believe it's finally here. I mean, think about it: this is our *last* first day of high school. This time next year, we'll be at college . . .'

Lee groaned. 'Don't remind me. I already had that speech off my mom this morning – complete with tearful eyes. I don't even want to *think* about college.'

'Tough luck, buddy. It's inevitable. We're moving up in the world.'

Even though the thought of college applications made my stomach twist, too; I'd tried to work on my application essay over the summer, but still hadn't made any progress on it.

I didn't even want to *think* about the possibility that Lee and I would end up at different colleges. That he'd get accepted somewhere I didn't. That we might end up apart next year. We'd spent our entire lives practically joined at the hip. What the hell would I do without him around?

'Unfortunately,' Lee was saying, drawing me out of my thoughts. 'Look, you're not going to start waxing lyrical about the future or something, are you? Please say if you are. I'll leave you to your thoughts and go find the guys.'

Playfully, I shoved my shoulder into his. 'I'll stop talking about college now. Promise.'

'Thank God for that.'

'Although, speaking of the guys – has Cam told you anything about this new neighbor?'

'I'd almost forgotten about that.'

Cam, one of our closest friends since elementary school, had sprung the news on us last week that some guy had moved into the house opposite his and, since he was our age, Cam's parents had suggested he take the new guy under his wing and introduce him to us – and the way Cam had said *suggested* made it sound like they'd given him an ultimatum about it.

Lee carried on. 'I know he's from Detroit. And his name's Levi. Like the jeans. I don't know much else

3

about him, though. I don't think Cam knows anything else about him, either, really.' Then he stood up off the Mustang. 'I'm just hoping he's not a total asshat, since we promised Cam we'd try and help him fit in. Help Levi fit in, I mean.'

'I know what you mean,' I mumbled, but I was distracted by my cell phone, which had started to ring in my hands.

Lee's gaze went to the caller ID, and he sighed. I looked up to give him an apologetic smile just in time to see him roll his eyes at me and start to stroll away, backpack slung over one shoulder.

'No phone sex, Shelly. This is a school. Keep it PG,' he said.

'Oh, like you and Rachel never made out in the janitor's closet!' I shot back. He just gave me a thumbs-up over his shoulder.

I answered the phone. 'Hey, Noah.'

Lee's older brother, Noah, was half the reason I'd not made progress on my college application essay: after sneaking around with him behind Lee's back for a couple of months last spring (which ended in total disaster when Lee caught us kissing), and then officially dating him since the summer, we'd spent as much of our vacation together as possible. He was in college at the other end of the country, now, at Harvard.

He'd been gone barely a couple of weeks, and I couldn't get over how much I missed him. How was I going to cope with not seeing him until Thanksgiving?

'Hey, how are you?'

'I'm good. Start of senior year excitement. How's college?'

'Eh. Not much different from when I called you last night. I had class this morning. Math. It was pretty interesting. Second-order differentials.'

'I have no idea what you're talking about, and I don't think I want to know.'

Noah laughed, a soft, breathy sort of chuckle that made my heart melt. Almost everything about him made my heart melt or my knees go weak or my stomach fill with butterflies. I was a goofball, a cliché straight out of a movie. And it felt great.

Have you read all

books?

THE KISSING BOOTH

When Elle decides to run a kissing booth for the school carnival, she never imagines she'll sit in it – or that her first ever kiss would be with bad boy Noah.

From that moment, her life is turned upside down – but is this a romance destined for happiness or heartbreak?

GOING THE DISTANCE

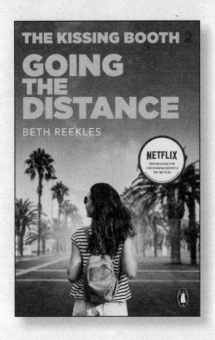

Elle seems to have finally tamed hotter-than-hot bad boy Noah Flynn, but now they're facing a new challenge. Noah's three thousand miles away at Harvard, and they're officially a long-distance couple.

Then she sees Noah getting friendly with another girl online, and a new cute boy at school shows interest in Elle.

With her heart on the line, what's a girl to do?

GOING THE DISTANCE